KOR
AND THE
WINGLESS
STRANGER

SANNA HINES

For Donna

CHAPTER ONE

The Wingless Boy

Father caught me staring up at my little brother and his friends playing air tag. Adom's speed and balance were perfect as he shot after his target.

"He looks good up there," Father said. "He'll be ready for next spring's Summit Flight competition."

"Adom will win." I pictured my family cheering him on from the starting line, shouting ourselves hoarse, urging him to reach the Cave of the Gods first so he'd get the blessing. I'd want him to win with all my heart—except that tiny, selfish part that would shrivel from shame if I hadn't had even one decent flight before my little brother became a hero. I lowered my head, and shoved my hands into my pockets.

"Look, son, you need to get back to flying."

My own Summit Flight last year ended after two wing beats and a splat on the sand. The bruises hurt less than the teasing that followed me ever since, so I kept my feet on the ground.

Father ran a hand through his thick crown feathers. "I didn't make it far on my own Summit Flight when I was fifteen. Couldn't fly well at that age. Still, when I got a little older, I made up for lost time." He grinned, flared out his great wings, then retracted them and tugged at my black, leading edge feathers. "All's not lost, Kor. Keep trying."

I'm taller than most. I knew building the muscle to raise my weight took time, but how much more time? Some days, it felt like I'd already lifted mountains.

After Father left for the hunt, I worked my chest and back muscles until they screamed at me to stop. Something inside insisted I go on, that I was nearly ready. I was hoping—really, *really* hoping—today would be my day for a real flight. If it wasn't, well, before dawn no one would see me fail again.

I waited through the night. It was still dark when I climbed down from the loft Adom and I shared to the other room of our home, the place where we ate and stored things and where my parents slept. My mother was alone, so I knew my father hadn't yet returned. Shoving aside the leather drape covering our doorway, I slipped outside and moved toward the roost platform.

Our tree is the tallest of the Hunters' Ring. From the roost, I could see most of Sea Grove. The walkways around trees and the bridges linking main branches were empty. Far below, the grounder stockade lay covered by its night net. The distant knoll where the Tropicals live was dim, unlit by glowpots. Even the tops of the walls surrounding Sea Grove looked deserted, patrolled only by pangolins. The guard animals prowled, sniffing here and there, not finding anything interesting enough to slow their pace.

All good. I wouldn't be mocked on my way down the ladder to the forest floor, the ropes stretched taut and the slats creaking under my weight. No one would call me "downy" or any other scatty name.

We use the area between inner and outer walls for flight training. I'd just gone through the seaside gate of the inner wall when I stopped. To the north, at the end of the long strip of open grass where I planned to practice flying, I spotted something odd. It was roughly half my height, shiny black, and shaped like an arrowhead.

Trap set by a raider scout? The arrowhead-thing wasn't big enough to hide a Tundran, so I moved closer.

Above me, I heard footsteps on the inner wall. I turned to see a face peek over the parapet edge. A small, wingless boy jumped down to stand beside me. He landed easily, not wincing or showing any sign of pain from the steep drop. Too young to be a raider, he didn't look like a threat. His clothing was all one piece, brown cloth tunic and trousers joined at the waist. He had fine fur of the same color on his head instead of feathers. I stared dumbly at a *furred* boy.

The boy pointed at the distant thing, then at his back, and made flapping motions with his arms. His arm flapping suggested to me that the arrowhead shape worked like wings for him. So maybe he flew in, left his strange wings on the grass, and then climbed up the wall to get a better look at the village.

But why? Nobody traveled alone. Even grown hunters flew together in casts, and they carried bow and arrows or spears. This boy had no weapons I could see and no companions.

The stranger stuck out his hand, gazing up at me with wide eyes. He waited a moment, then pulled back the hand, snapped his feet together, and bowed.

I'm a Woodlander, not a Tropical, with their bowing and titles and haughty ways! Was he a fool? Where had this boy come from that he didn't know how to behave?

When I held up my fist in greeting, he edged away, growling noises I couldn't understand. His speech sounded like a stomach rumbling. I told him my name and asked for his. He didn't answer but seemed to decide I wasn't trouble, and so he relaxed.

Or he tried to relax, anyway. When he shifted his feet, he staggered. He looked surprised by this. Hands shoving the fringe of fur away from his eyes, the boy rubbed the skin of his face. Then his eyes rolled back, and he fell to the ground.

In a near panic, I looked around for anyone who could help. What I really needed was a priest from the Order of Gray. A Gray would know what to do. I'd have to run to the temple as fast as I could. If my stupid wings worked, I could fly there in no time, but running might take too long. Whatever ailed the furred boy looked serious.

I stood over him as he thrashed on the ground. His body shook and his mouth opened and closed like a fish on land. I had to do something soon.

The wind was strong. *Maybe...maybe I can glide a bit—just a little bit—over to where his strange wings are. Maybe something there will help him.*

I bent to pick him up. He'd stopped moving, and so wasn't too hard to lift, but he felt surprisingly heavy in my arms. I unfurled my wings, flexing them. The breeze caught and held against my secondaries. With a silent prayer to the gods I wouldn't crash, I ran to gain speed and launched myself into the wind.

Flapping like mad, I wasn't exactly flying but doing more of a hover sort of thing. All right, it wasn't even that, yet my feet left the ground and I didn't fall over. Every now and then, I had to bounce away from the grass, but I covered the distance to the stranger's wings much faster than at a run. If I hadn't been so worried about the boy, I'd have felt great.

I set him down and poked at his wings, getting more and more confused. They had straps to fit a body, but I couldn't picture how the wings might bend. There was only one, solid piece made of nothing I'd seen before. Smooth as polished wood, the surface had no grain. It was harder than rubber and lighter than firestone.

Then I saw her. As if I needed more trouble, coming toward me was the unmistakable shape of Ilyssa Too. Ilyssa was the proudest girl in Sea Grove. Maybe she had reason to be. She was a Tropical, and she was pretty. Ilyssa had big, brown eyes, a straight, little nose, and a mouth that curled up at the corners. There wasn't even a tinge of yellow in her pure white feathers. With the sun rising, glazing her primaries and the edges of her white clothes, she looked like a sky goddess.

Ilyssa was the best flyer of anyone our age, last year's Summit Flight champion. As she drifted expertly to the grass beside me, I hoped she hadn't seen me crow hop through my flight.

"Kor Tiercel?" She looked from me to the furred boy to the wings. "What's going on?"

"I found this stranger. I can't say how he got here, but I think he used these odd wings somehow."

"Why does he have fur instead of feathers?"

"Ilyssa, I don't know!"

She stared at me, shocked. Her crest feathers arched forward.

I remembered my manners. "Miss Too," I said quickly, "he's in trouble. He couldn't breathe, and then he went to sleep."

She tapped a finger on her lips, eyes studying the boy. "I had a problem on my Summit Flight. The higher up the mountain I flew, the harder it was to breathe. Kor, look for a mask."

"A mask?"

"Yes. Search for something to fit over his face. I'll fan him with my wings."

I saw an object lying beside the wings that might be a mask. It looked like sheet ice wrapped in rubber, and it had long tubes attached to a square box. I was nervous about touching the thing, but I didn't want Ilyssa to think I was afraid, so I picked it up. It wasn't cold.

"Hold the mask over his face," Ilyssa said.

I did. I heard a hissing sound, and the furred boy's chest moved up and down. He opened his eyes, pulled the mask's band around the back of his head, and then lay back.

Ilyssa and I watched him breathe. "How did you know about the mask?" I asked.

"I used one after my Summit Flight."

I nodded, knowing she could say no more. Only the champion of the Flight is allowed to learn from the gods, and yet Ilyssa said, "On the mountain, I got dizzier and dizzier until I reached the Cave of the Gods. I don't remember going in. I must have fallen asleep. When I woke, there was a mask over my face, and I felt better. That's how I knew." Ilyssa smiled at me. "I've never told anyone else about that."

Of all the things that happened during the morning, Ilyssa Too's smile surprised me most. As I said, I'm Woodlander and she's Tropical, but just then, who we were didn't matter.

She looked down at the boy. "He's awake, and he isn't struggling. I think he's better. We should take him to the temple. The Grays will know what he is. Carry him, won't you?"

Scat! What to do? I wouldn't—*couldn't*—admit I didn't trust my flying. "Um, it might not be safe to move him," I hedged.

"Well, not with your wings held in tight like you did before," Ilyssa observed. "Can't get enough lift that way. You'll really have to stretch full out, you know, but you have huge wings. I'm sure he'll be fine with you."

Ilyssa Too thought I had *huge* wings. I picked up the boy, barely noticing his weight. My eyes were on Ilyssa as she took off, a pearly cloud against the pink, morning sky. I stretched my huge wings, felt the wind hold me, and flew toward the shadowed temple of the Grays.

6

CHAPTER TWO

Sea Grove

"*Ilyssa Too?*" Jass choked out. He clutched hands over his heart, pretending to reel with shock. His clowning made the rope bridge beneath our feet sway. I grabbed the handrail. Jass laughed.

We'd been best friends since we both lived on the lowest branches of the same tree. He knew me better than anyone, but I hadn't told him about my flight. Jass was such a good flyer, I wanted to get in more practice before I tried to keep up with him.

He elbowed my ribs. "Next thing we know, you'll be visiting the Tropical knoll, sipping mango juice while lounging in one of their fabulous rainwater pools...."

I scowled at him. Mocking my favorite daydream made me crazy, which was why he kept at it. How many nights had we perched on the roost, imagining life among the Tropicals, even plotting to spy on their splendor? But that wouldn't happen.

"As if," I snarled. Woodlanders and Tropicals didn't mix.

Before the Tropicals appeared in our zone, Woodlander hunters and foragers shared the grove of great trees. Foragers are smaller than hunters and they eat what they can find, so everyone got along. None of us had any use for grounders, heavy people whose habit of nesting below the trees blocked game trails and attracted dangerous myrmecs.

Then the Tropicals showed up, bringing rubber tubes to move water and waste so Woodlanders could live closer together. They taught us to build walls around the grove and to make nets to repel insect swarms. More of us survived, so not everyone needed to search for food. The extras made goods to send with caravans the Tropicals conducted between our zone and their empire to the south.

And it was the Tropicals who convinced us to open our grove to the grounders, saying they could be useful for clearing the forest floor of leaves and needles. Piles of these packed tight would give off heat to rise through bamboo pipes. After that, our homes were warmer, and the great wildfires that once burned from sea to mountains became only memories.

Last of all came the Order of Gray, priests of the Tropicals, and their stone gods who needed a temple, though our gods always heard us when we spoke to them in the open air. We built the temple, and the Grays lived there, keeping lists of their gods' many rules on wooden tablets no one else could read. They knew things, the Grays, and so we took them problems we couldn't solve, like we did today when Ilyssa and I found the wingless boy.

Jass was still in a teasing mood. His orange eyes glittered as he said, "When it comes to getting a girl's attention, plumage isn't everything. Sneakiness can make up for a lot. I found out the Too family is having a party for the older daughter tonight. Ilyssa's sister is engaged to one of the Tropicals who came with the caravan yesterday. Maybe you'll be invited to the party?"

"Enough!" I yelled. Then I lowered my voice. "How do you know about this party?"

"My sister's serving her best wines, and she's made some nibbles to go with. Want to dress up as servers?"

"That's the stupidest idea ever."

"Hey, no one's making you do it, but I'll be here at the bridge around six." Jass shrugged, and then asked, "So what about this furred creature? What will the Grays do with it?"

I snorted. "Why would the Grays tell me anything?"

"Figured you might get a reward or something, seeing as it's such a curiosity. I've heard they've moved the creature's wings inside both walls and put a guard on them."

"No! Why?"

Jass mimicked my voice. "Why would the Grays tell me anything?" He wrinkled his snub nose and laughed. His laughter cut off when a flicker of fire crackled high overhead. He followed the smoke trail with his eyes. "Gods!" Jass jumped at the boom of following thunder. "Could be a wild night, maybe even a firefall. Wouldn't that be great?"

I squinted at him. "Do you *want* Sea Grove to burn?"

"No firestorm's going to destroy our grove. It's been here forever. I wouldn't mind a little damage if they'd have to build new nesting areas just in time for us to move up."

I thought about that. When we turned seventeen, we'd join the singlets on the highest branches of our trees. I wasn't looking forward to moving up the way Jass was. I was afraid I'd be homesick for my parents and brother. Jass lived with his sister, Sea Grove's winemaker, in a nest overcrowded with her brood. He was more than ready to be on his own.

He swung a leg casually over the bridge handrail and stepped away to hover on air, held up by a few strong beats of his wings. "You really must get airborne soon," he told me with a wink, "or I'll have all the girls to myself."

Jass sailed down from our ring of tall trees, past the dense tangle of the grounders' thicket to disappear behind their stockade. A short-winged grounder girl on the forest floor stared after him, mouth open. Seconds later, Jass looped back through the branches above my head.

"Later," he called, and then he was gone.

My brother was playing ball with some friends on the roost by our nest. Adom looked busy with the game, so I just waved as I approached from the bridge and would have gone on, but he caught the ball and said, "Kor! Tell us about this beast you found."

I shook my head. "He's no beast. He's like us, except he's wingless, small, and furred."

"Is it an elf?" one of the friends asked. She had the ruddy crown and the pointy, spotted wings of a smaller hunter.

Adom turned to the girl with scorn. "There are no elves, Kes. That's just stories. Right, Kor?"

"Whatever he is, he's real enough."

"Cursed by the gods to live without wings," a dark-skinned forager boy said gravely. Smaller than the others, his feathers were thick and shiny black. "This stranger must have done something terrible."

I held out my hands. I'm no expert on the gods. "That's for the Grays to decide."

The forager looked unsatisfied, but I couldn't help him. I said, "The boy is at the temple. If you want to know more, you should ask someone there," and I lifted the drape to my nest.

The rest of the day passed badly. My mother fussed over me, afraid I'd caught mites from the stranger. She preened my feathers until my father returned from the hunt, worried about…well, I didn't know. He kept asking questions. I told him my story twice, but that wasn't enough.

"You're sure, Kor, you haven't left anything out?"

"I've told you *everything*." My voice was sour with exasperation. Did he think I was so downy I could forget what happened only hours ago?

My father sat on his stool and said, "It's just that, in all my flights, I've never seen anything like what you describe. Where could it have come from? What is it?"

"*He*. It's a *he*," I said, now sounding sullen and downy, even to myself.

Mother came to my rescue. She handed Father a cup of wine and said, "Tamm, let it go. Kor doesn't know more than he's told you. The Grays will learn the truth and then explain it to us, don't you think? Everybody's wondering about this thing. We know it's—*he's*," she corrected herself, glancing in my direction, "not Tropical or Woodlander, unless he's some odd type of Chiro."

Father shook his head. "Chiros stay in their caves during the day, and even their youngest have wings. They're born winged."

Mother grimaced. "It's hard enough to give birth to a wingless chick. I'm glad I'm not a Chiro."

"So am I," Father returned, grinning at her.

My mother wasn't in the mood for humor. She frowned. "If he isn't a Chiro, how can he have fur on his head? Could he be from the far, far north, maybe even the top of the Tundra zone? Perhaps chicks there grow out their wings later than ours because they have less to eat."

I thought about the mask that looked like ice and the slick surface of the black wings. The furred boy might have come from somewhere up north.

Gnawing his lip, my father considered my mother's words. "That's possible." His face turned guarded and grim. "With the cold getting worse each year, a lot of creatures are on the move. Tundran hunters have pushed south into our zone. There was news of them...."

He shared a look with my mother. It was one of those not-in-front-of-the-chicks looks. I was supposed to pretend I hadn't seen it, but this time, I wanted to hear the rest.

"A raid?" I asked boldly.

Father took a long breath. After a moment, he said, "Yes. You're flying again—and I'm so proud of you, son. We'll have a feast tomorrow to celebrate—but now, I suppose you're old enough to know the whole truth. A small grove five days' flight from here was attacked, the adults killed, and the chicks taken for slaves."

"That close?" Mother whispered.

"We're well defended, Miriah. Our walls are strong, our—"

"The walls are only meant to turn back insect swarms—myrmecs and coleos. People can fly in from overhead."

"We have the nets and a good number of hunters."

"Tundran hunters are *monsters*!" Mother wailed. "Sea Grove has too many grounders and Tropicals. What use will they be in a fight?"

"The Tropicals are clever. The grounders are strong," Father said. "We can ask the Shore folk from the cove to help us, too."

"Shores don't care about land," my mother scoffed. "They'll just leave if it gets dangerous here."

Father sighed. "That, too, is possible." He slapped his hands on his thighs. "What's for supper, woman?" he asked in a falsely hearty voice. "And where is our Adom?"

I slipped out after I finished eating, hiding my best tunic under my ordinary clothes. Father wouldn't like the idea of my pretending to be a servant. He'd say that wasn't dignified. I didn't want to argue with him; I wanted to find Jass. Visiting the Tropical knoll, even as a server for a party, was too good a chance to miss.

Jass waited for me by the bridge, smoothing the white patches above his ears. He was always preening those feathers because he thought they made him look older. Like his flight feathers, the side streaks had come in early. "The white looks good against the dark gray of my crown, doesn't it? Girls like contrast," he told me once. I dunno. I'm not a girl. Jass always looked like Jass to me.

"You ready?" he asked.

"I think so." Pulling off my everyday tunic, I stuffed this under an arm and posed in my black one for Jass' approval. He nodded.

"Is it all right with your sister that I help at the party?" I asked.

"She kissed my cheek, she was so happy to have extra hands. I'm her favorite brother just now."

"You're her only brother."

"True. And isn't she lucky to have me?"

I groaned as Jass lifted his smug chin, but soon we were off to get casks at the winery, and from there, we were going to the Tropical knoll!

CHAPTER THREE

The Knoll

When we reached the bridge to the knoll, I whispered to Jass, "This place is fantastic."

"Quit gawking. Keep walking." Jass hustled me along the bridge over the ravine. We were late. It took extra time to reach the Toos' villa because we hiked like nestlings. I hadn't yet told Jass I'd flown. The truth was I didn't trust my wings to carry me and the heavy wine cask.

The Toos' tree stood closest to the sea. Their villa filled three full branches, I'd heard. There were only four in the family: Ilyssa, her parents, and an older sister named Sorlyn. What did they do with so much space?

It was windier near the coastal rise, but the view of the water was spectacular. The tree leaned away from onshore breezes, forcing me to watch my footing as we crossed the slanted last bridge, an arbor decorated with captive fireflies. Clay shields sheltered the insects from wind. The arbor ended at a landing platform with a gate. Behind the gate, a grounder wearing Too livery—a white tunic edged with yellow—took one look at us and jerked a thumb toward the platform. "Deliveries in back."

"But we're servers," Jass protested.

"Aren't we all?" the guard said in a bored voice.

"These casks are heavy and my friend doesn't fly," Jass argued before I could stop him.

The guard stared up at me and burst into laughter. "And they call us grounders flightless! Here, then, downies, hand those over." He reached toward my burden. "Go back across the arbor, and you'll find a chick ladder to the forest floor. Walk to the rear of this tree, and there will be another ladder to climb up. You'll be safe enough on those."

I could feel my face flushing. "No," I husked at the guard. "I can fly." Jass stared at me, his expression asking what game I was playing. I was too embarrassed to explain.

Clamping my arms around the wine cask, I marched to the end of the flight platform and looked toward the black waves of the sea. The breeze whipped my crown feathers every which way; there was no steadiness to the wind's direction. If I got hit with a down blast, I'd drop like a stone. The best I could do was to improve my ruddering, so I put down the cask to untie my breech cuffs, freeing my shin feathers.

Jass asked, "You're going to fly? You're really going to do it?"

I nodded vigorously, squaring my shoulders. "Yes."

He drew back with a skeptical look, but seconds later, he yanked his ties free and shouted, "Come on! Let's show that grounder what hunters can do." As he hurled himself off the platform, he made a rude noise at the guard. Then he was past the rise and the walls, past beach and sandbar, doing rolls and flips while I nudged my toes over the platform's edge. I saw fireflicks on the horizon, which looked very far away.

I was going to die.

I fell. Terrified, I hugged the cask hard, and my wings tucked in along with my arms. I fell faster. A crosswind hit me, sending me up, and in that instant, my stubbornness took over: I would *not* die in front of Ilyssa Too's tree. Not me. Not tonight.

Whoosh. Fury and fear sent my wings out with a snap. Astonished by my own reaction, I was jerked upward and my wings held. I countered the updraft with a few hard pulls, and I was above the water *soaring*. The morning's short sail from practice slope to temple was nothing, nothing like this. I threw back my head and howled. I was one with the sky. I was riding the wind. I was—

Jass smacked a wing tip across the back of my head. "You've been holding out on me," he growled.

I banked to face to him. "This is new today."

"Woohoo!" he cried, happily now. "Kor Tiercel flies! Look out, world."

Distracted by Jass, I sank too near the waves. Spray splashed my legs, spattering my shin feathers. It was time to stop fooling around. I signaled to Jass, and we made for the lee side of the Toos' tree.

Panting hard, I landed on the back platform. Getting there was tricky, as we had to thread through dense branches. We set down our casks and straightened our clothing. Jass pounded my back. I grinned at him. We were equals again.

There was another guard at the back gate, but this one didn't have the fancy tunic. He grunted when he saw us, handed us a glow bucket to light our way, and then sent us along a main limb wide enough for a fern and orchid garden to cover the bark. The wind's roaring was muted along the mossy path. It was quiet except for shell chimes tinkling somewhere. Tiny, silver frogs skittered away from us. A collared snake glided down from a vine and whipped after them.

We emerged from the path into a gap between limbs with a rainwater pool wedged between them. Jass caught my arm and we fell back into shadow for a better look. Though we'd tried to imagine what such things were like, we never thought of a lake in a tree. The pond was twice as wide as a man is tall and many times as long, edged with blue-green stone brought up from below so it looked like a tidal pool. The moon's reflection floated on its still surface.

Spaces between other broad limbs of the Toos' tree were floored by planks, making porches where a person could walk or sit, places like the roost near my nest, but bigger, and prettier. There were tall boxes planted with flowers and low ones holding squares of short-cut grass. Carved wooden benches were thick with colorful pillows.

Against the tree trunk, a villa rose through to the next two levels of branches. Its walls were bamboo, and its roof was made of clay tiles. Someone has painted symbols in swirling, flowery Tropical script on a birch banner above the back entrance. The banner seemed festive, welcoming.

Ilyssa came out from the villa to stand looking into the pool. She was wearing white shimmery stuff, fine as nid silk. Pearls twined through her crest; the largest was teardrop shaped and hung over her forehead. She turned away from the water when a servant in livery approached.

Jass whistled softly, and I got mad. Who was Jass Gos to be whistling at Ilyssa Too? I was about to slam back a sharp remark when he added, "Will you look at the shin feathers on *that* one."

I stared at him. "What are you talking about? She's in a gown."

"Gown? Oh, you mean Ilyssa. She looks nice tonight, but that other girl is amazing. I didn't expect a Tundran grounder here, especially one with such fine, fine plumage." Jass tilted his head while he sized up the servant girl, whose coloring *was* pretty—rusty crown feathers with red combs just behind each temple. Her wings shaded from white to brown to dark orange. I guessed her to have a couple of years on us. I'd seen her in the market with Ilyssa.

"That's Ilyssa's new servant," I informed Jass, "and we're here to work like she is, so we'd better get to it. Your sister will pluck us if we show up any later."

We moved into the open and Ilyssa beckoned to us, giving our casks and clothing the once-over with her eyes. "Kor? You're here as a *server*?"

"Yes, er, Miss Ilyssa."

She accepted this use of her first name with just the barest lift of one eyebrow. I dipped my head, ready to go into the villa, but she asked, "Do you know what happened to the wingless boy?"

"No, do you?"

Her crest arched forward—I'd forgotten to add the "Miss" part—but she said, "All I've heard is he's still at the temple. Wish I knew for certain he was all right."

Jass stepped forward. "Well now, Miss Too, you might go over and inquire."

"You're...?"

"Jass Gos. We were in the same Lore class."

"Oh, yes. I remember," Ilyssa said, but her blank expression wasn't convincing. I was pleased she'd forgotten Jass. Other Tropical girls still smiled at him when they passed, though our Lore classes together ended more than a year ago. For several moons, the Grays taught all the fledglings preparing for Summit Flights about the Tropical gods. After that, we Woodlanders went back to learning hunting or trades from our elders. Tropicals got more schooling from their own kind, I'd heard.

"I couldn't leave to check on the boy," Ilyssa went on, her face pointed toward the temple so she was talking more to herself than to Jass or me. "Guests are arriving. My parents expect me to stay. I'm supposed to meet one of Ferd Mac's cousins, and—"

The servant girl interrupted. I wished she hadn't; I wanted to know more about this cousin. "You two," she instructed Jass and me, "take that wine through the back door immediately. The other server is in the larder." She pointed and looked stern, so I did as told, but when I glanced back at Jass, who lagged behind me on the way to the back door, I caught him winking at her.

Jass' sister grabbed him by the ear the instant he entered the larder. "Where have you been?" Ida Gos shrieked, releasing Jass with a shove before she took his cask. She took mine next, setting them beside others on a table. "Jass, peel the seals off these, pour the wine into goblets, and start passing out drinks. Kor, offer this food around." She thrust platters of glazed fruits and nuts at me.

The main room was such a shock that I stood there, trays in hand, gaping like a nestling. This was the biggest room I'd ever seen. It curved to follow the tree limb beneath, but the bark of the branch had been cut away and the wood sealed with resin. Above this gleaming floor, the furniture was made of vines braided together in complicated patterns. Glowpots shaded by seashells were everywhere.

The color was overwhelming. It's easy to forget how bright Tropicals are because they so often wear dull cloaks against the cold or maybe to look more like the rest of us. Tonight, they were in their glory, draped in robes and gowns of the same glossy stuff Ilyssa wore, and each person's colors matched his plumage.

A picture came into my mind: I saw my Woodlander ancestors gazing at these brilliant newcomers when the Tropicals first appeared in our zone. How awed they must have been.

As I held out my trays to guests, my eyes searched for Ilyssa. One minute she was talking with her parents, and the next, she danced with a green Tropical. Again, I was struck by the oddness of their ways, for when Tropicals danced, they used only their feet and hands, keeping their wings tight behind them. Our dances are riotous things, held under the noon sun or on a full-moon night, when young Woodlander males soar above land and sea, showing their power and plumage to the ladies while drums pound and horns blare.

Trays empty, I returned to the larder. Where was Jass? Ida threw up her hands, clucking in disgust about "shiftless, good-for-nothing, lazy fools."

Hefting a wine tray, I slunk away. If I knew Jass—and I did know Jass—he'd be off somewhere with Ilyssa's pretty servant. When I needed refills again, Ida was gone. So, like shiftless Jass, I slipped out the back door to explore more of the Tropicals' luxurious world.

I was admiring the rainwater pool when I heard a noise by the moss path. A cloaked figure carrying a huge shell was stealing toward the back gate. Without thinking, I plunged after the thief.

CHAPTER FOUR

Forest Floor

I caught hold of the cloak, and the thief whirled on me. My fingers flew away from the leather.

"What are you doing?" Ilyssa hissed.

"I thought you were a *thief.*"

She shifted the horn-shaped triton shell over to one hip and glared. It was strange to see her wearing baggy, grounder clothes. They were bunched up, and through the open neck of the tunic, I saw the edge of her gown.

"Well, I'm not a thief." Ilyssa's eyes narrowed. "You're taking time from work to look around, aren't you? You're no better than that other boy who went somewhere with Mellora."

"Mellora?"

"My servant." Ilyssa rolled her eyes. "Isn't anyone doing what he's supposed to be doing?" Suddenly, she laughed and shook her head. "No, I guess not."

Encouraged by her change of mood, I asked, "Where are you going? Is the party over?"

"It's just getting started. I'm counting on it lasting for hours yet so I'll have time for…well, for…oh, never mind. Go back to your work." Ilyssa strode away, but I was right on her heels. She turned, saying, "Go. Shoo!" and flicked her wrists at me.

"You shouldn't be by yourself," I warned. "Not everyone in the grove is peaceable on a Saturday night after the wine starts flowing."

"I'm just going to the temple. It's a short flight. And besides, I don't have to explain myself to you."

"Your disguise won't work. Grounders don't wear pearls," I reminded her.

"Oh!" Her free hand pulled the forehead bangle out from her feathers. Shoving the jewelry into a pocket, she looked flustered for a moment before she collected herself and lifted her chin.

"I do *not* need an escort," Ilyssa insisted. I was reminded of my brother when he wanted something he wasn't supposed to have. He stamped his foot the way she was doing, and pouted afterward, just as she did next. "Besides, I can't find Mellora."

"I'll go with you."

Ilyssa gaped at me. "You? But you're a server."

"Just for tonight. I'll be joining a hunting cast soon," I told her proudly. "So how about it? Will I do as escort?"

She looked at me, at the path, and finally, at the branches overhead. She sighed. "All right. No, wait. If people see me with you, they'll think we're sneaking out together. That would be terrible. I'd be in such trouble."

Now I was the one looking down and up nervously. "I'll stay back a ways but keep an eye on you. If there's any trouble, I'll come to your rescue."

"You forget how well I fly!" Ilyssa declared.

"You forget how pretty you are!" The second that came out of my mouth, I wanted to drown myself in the sea. *I am so stupid. How will I ever—*

"You really think so?" Ilyssa inquired.

"I…I…mean, you're easy to spot, even at night. The way you fly is so different, so graceful. You're…." I gave up, exhaled heavily, and shook my head. I'd made a complete fool of myself. My cheeks were burning.

"Kor," Ilyssa said after a pause, and I looked up, startled, when she used my name, "let's go to the temple now, all right? Just stay behind me."

We had to pass the guard to fly from the rear platform, and I worried that he might try to stop us from leaving together, but Ilyssa ducked into the ferns before we reached him. The branches near the outside of the tree were too thick to fly through. When Ilyssa dropped through the foliage, I thought she'd fallen, but no, she waved at me from the next level down as though she'd done this before.

I followed her from branch to branch until we came to lowest bridge between trees, but she didn't cross; instead, she searched along the trunk for something. Her hand closed on the ties for a chick ladder that had been hauled up for the night. The ladder fell with a noisy thud to the ground. She set a foot on the first slat.

I called to her, "You're not going down *there*."

"You're right about my being easy to see at night. There are no homes below. If I stay cloaked and on foot, no one will notice us go by," she explained as she descended.

I stared into the darkness at the base of the tree, shivering from the thought of venturing into the forbidden realm. All my life, my parents warned me about the forest floor at night. I told myself no insect swarms had been spotted this moon, and I shouldn't behave like a trembling downy. Those thoughts helped a little, but my heart still pounded when my feet touched the spongy turf.

Night fog was thick around us. We had a long way to go in this darkness. The Tropical knoll ran along the north edge of Sea Grove while the temple stood by the southwest corner. Though Ilyssa was only a few paces ahead, I'd have lost her if it weren't for her white crest. I wondered how we'd find our way to the temple until I heard her shaking something, and then a faint, blue light came on.

"Is that a glowrod?" I whispered, awestruck. I've heard of them, of course, but I'd never seen one up close. I didn't get to inspect the glowrod then, either, because Ilyssa was moving quickly, and I couldn't lag too far behind.

"What's that *smell*?" she whispered after a minute.

"The heat pits," I guessed, though it might have been the grounders' waste dump. As it turned out, I was wrong. We'd wandered too close to a glypto corral. The glowrod saved me from stumbling into the trench around the livestock. Most of the glyptos were sleeping, but one old bull, whose shell was thickly crusted with lichen, lifted his bony head and eyed me suspiciously. He thunked his spiked tail in warning, waking the others who made low, complaining grunts as they pulled in their heads and feet to become living boulders. I backed away, trying not to disturb the giant animals further.

Ilyssa paused to get her bearings. Everything looked so different at night. The grounder thicket was just ahead, but I didn't suppose we'd run into anyone. Their stockade was sealed at this hour, its rows of barbed pikes and overhead netting protecting the people inside. I could see a few lights beyond the stockade walls and hear voices and music, but just as I suspected, when we skirted the area of low trees and shrubs they favor, we were alone except for a sizable manylegs, one of the biggest I'd ever seen, longer than my arm. Ilyssa held very still when she saw it and bit her lip, but the crawler wasn't interested in us. It burrowed into leaf mold.

The Hunters' Ring rose to our left. I warned Ilyssa to hide the light and to pull up the hood of her cloak. As she did that, I looked toward the roost by my family's home, smirking at my memory of the times I'd perched there with Jass, trying to imagine what Tropicals did on Saturday nights. Now I knew: They sneaked around on the forest floor.

We turned toward the sea to approach the temple, which sat on a platform supported by posts three times a man's height. I expected Ilyssa to uncloak and fly up to the courtyard. The courtyard held shrines to the thirteen Tropical gods, one for each moon of the year. Unlike our old gods, who are always there guarding our trees, these new ones only paid attention to us during the moon when they got their gifts. This was the ninth moon, so the ninth god—a fellow named Geen—was awake just now, but why he would want Ilyssa's big shell, I couldn't imagine.

She didn't make for the courtyard, moving instead around the base of the structure, studying stone blocks that closed the space between posts. The blocks had been set without mortar, so there were gaps between them. Every now and then, Ilyssa stopped near a chink in the enclosure, holding her ear to the pointed end of the shell.

Finally, I could stand it no longer. "What *are* you doing?"

"Listening. I think I can hear him."

"Him?" Of course! When we brought the furred boy here, the Grays talked about taking him "below." He'd be in this space beneath the temple. "You want to listen to *him*?"

"Shh." Ilyssa held a finger to her lips, and then she touched the shell to the wall again. After a while, she handed me the shell.

I couldn't do anything with it until Ilyssa shoved my head to the side and the tip of the horn wedged in my ear. Hollow sounds of several voices came through to me. It wasn't the boy, for these voices spoke our language. I had to be hearing some of the Grays.

"I tell you we *must* do it," First Voice, a man, said. "A fall from the cliffs…an accident."

"A sacrifice to Geen?" Second Voice, a woman, suggested.

In the silence that followed, Ilyssa tried to pry the shell from my hands, but I resisted. I wanted to hear more. She tucked in, her ear against mine, so she could hear, too. I was so rattled to be that near her, I nearly forgot about the Grays, but she didn't; she gripped the shell until her knuckles went white.

The voices talked about the cliffs and the sea. First Voice wanted to be sure the water would "take it away." Second Voice said not to worry as long as the tide was going out.

Next thing I heard was the furred boy, who rumbled something in that strange speech of his. The sounds were deep, hoarse and slow.

Putting the shell under an arm, Ilyssa tugged on my sleeve and dragged me away from the wall to a place where we could talk.

"They're going to kill him," she whispered urgently.

"What has he done?"

"I don't think he's done anything. It's what he *is* that's the problem. Wingless, furred people don't make sense. They don't fit the Lore. The Grays are supposed to explain him; everyone's expecting that."

Ilyssa's dark eyes flashed anger. "They don't know what he is even though Grays are supposed to know everything, so they're desperate to be rid of him. You heard that part about the cliffs. They mean to push him off."

I gasped. "But he can't fly!"

CHAPTER FIVE

The Temple

Two big strigs swooped down from the temple platform. I hadn't given a thought to guards, and from the look on Ilyssa's face, neither had she. Strigs are only awake at night, and I'd always been to the temple during the day. Now here they were, still as huge, brown statues, arms crossed, staring down at us with their great, golden eyes.

"State your business," the bigger one said. His ear tufts stood straight up, thick and impressive.

"I must visit the temple," Ilyssa told him.

"At this hour?" the guard sneered.

Ilyssa shoved back her hood. Her crest arced forward. "Do you know who I am?"

The strig looked from her dusty boots to her upturned nose. He blinked slowly and said, "No."

"I am Miss Ilyssa Too, daughter of The Honorable Aurelius Too."

Clearly surprised, the first guard turned to the second, who had black braid on his tunic shoulders. This one stepped forward to ask, "So, Miss Too, what brings you here?"

"Are you deaf?" she barked. "I wish to make an offering."

"I can do that for you," the guard offered pleasantly.

"This shell—" Ilyssa thrust it out at him so he could see it better, "has great value. I will make the offering myself."

"And what of your escort?"

"My *servant* is of no account," Ilyssa said dismissively. "He is here only to protect me."

"Then here he will remain," the guard said.

Ilyssa stated firmly, "Kor will accompany me."

The strig changed tack. "Since your offering is so valuable, you would do better to return in the morning when the Gray Ones are not absorbed in meditation and can greet you properly."

"I am here now. Announce me."

The guards looked at each other. No words passed between them as the bulky one rubbed his nose while the other fingered his braid. The second one's ear tufts rose. "Impossible," he said finally. "We can't disturb them."

"*You* can't. *I* can," Ilyssa asserted. "I am a Summit Flight champion. I have been *called*." She challenged the two pairs of enormous eyes, holding their gaze without wavering. Faced with this determined, queenly girl, the guards crumbled visibly.

I was so shocked I turned my head to keep them from seeing my expression. After their experience at the Cave of the Gods, champions were sometimes drawn to the temple—"called," they said—and there they stayed for days, if not weeks. Could this have happened to Ilyssa?

"As you wish," the leader mumbled at last.

Ilyssa nodded. She tugged at her cloak ties and turned her back to me. We all stood there until I realized I was supposed to take the cloak. I lifted it off her awkwardly, but the guards didn't comment. They probably assumed I was dim. Why else would a hunter become a servant? I left my mouth shut to keep them thinking I was stupid.

Then, scat! Ilyssa stretched her wings high and lifted on the first beat.

It was such a swift, powerful move, my mouth hung open, making me look even dimmer. The guards were a full two beats behind, reaching the platform after she'd already landed.

Ilyssa waved an impatient hand at me. I took a deep breath. Could I copy that move? No, I didn't dare. Instead, I flapped flat half a dozen times, but got there all the same. A small jolt of pride shot through me. No more chick ladders for Kor Tiercel!

The black-braided guard went into the temple. The bigger one retreated to a niche by a wall. Ilyssa placed her shell on Geen's altar, then waited there, eying the temple door.

Two Grays, a man and a woman, came out. Grays always look old, even the chicks, because their eyes are white as their crowns, their wings are dust-colored, and they nearly always wear long, drab robes that cover their red shin feathers. Even so, these two seemed more ancient than the grove.

"You have returned to us so soon, Miss Too?" the man said.

That was the voice we'd heard through the temple walls. I hadn't recognized it as belonging to the Gray we'd met when we brought in the furred boy. Maybe the priest had forgotten me and would believe Ilyssa's story?

My heart sank when the woman—yes, that was Second Voice— added, "I see your companion of this morning is here, as well."

Now what were we to do?

There was a deep-throated bellow from the forest floor and then another—sounds of frightened beasts. Next came crashes and alarmed bawling as more excited animals joined in. Glowpots arose in the grounder thicket, along with shouts and curses.

Everyone moved close to the courtyard's edge to squint into the darkness. "The glyptos are loose," a strig guard reported.

This was bad. It was nearly impossible to stop a two-ton glypto that wanted to go somewhere. Generally, they didn't, being content to eat the grass their keepers supplied. The corral trench had been dug at a steep angle that was supposed to keep them in.

"How?" the Gray woman shrieked. "Why?"

She had her answers immediately. Lightning cracked overhead, releasing fiery streamers cascading downward, each ripple gathering into a ball that exploded when it hit trees or the thicket. It was bright enough now to see grounders running for cover. Glowpots poked out from branches in the Hunters' Ring, and I watched my people taking to the air, fire shields and flame beaters in their hands.

"Firefall. Into the temple," the Gray man commanded. "On the lowest level, we'll be safe from the bursts."

"No," I objected, forgetting that I was supposed to be a stupid servant. "My parents are on the fire squad. I should help them. I—"

"Kor!" Ilyssa cried, seizing my arm. "Stay." She lowered her voice to a whisper, "*Please*. Remember why we came."

I knew my duty was with my people, but I also knew that Ilyssa needed me. She wasn't afraid for herself; I could see that in her eyes. She was thinking about the furred boy. Just then, I didn't care about him all that much.

But she did, and I wondered if I should, too. There were flyers enough to deal with an ordinary firefall, and I wasn't trained for the work. The boy had no one to defend him. He didn't deserve to die just because he was different. Confused, I found myself rushing toward the temple entrance.

I'd never been inside the temple, and I'd never talked to anyone who had been. The main room was big but lit only by one small glowpot. Along the far wall, shelves held strangely shaped objects. Tall stacks of wooden tablets stood to my left. I was peering at a wall painting of Vala, the mountain with the Cave of the Gods, when a huge explosion outside shook the temple and made me jump.

Ilyssa crest went flat as she wailed in downy voice, "I want to be safe. Now!"

The Grays exchanged a look. "Of course," the man said. "Come this way."

We went through an arch and around a corner to wait there while the temple guard lifted the hatch to a ladder leading down. The Gray woman pulled a glowrod from her pocket, shook it, and handed it to Ilyssa, motioning her ahead. I wound Ilyssa's cloak around my left arm so it wouldn't tangle in my legs on the way down.

We reached a stone chamber with a gravel floor. There were no openings except for the hatch, so it was very dark. Ilyssa held out her light, revolving slowly in place until we spotted the furred boy huddled in a corner. He looked so small and miserable, I turned to make an angry complaint to the Grays, expecting them to be just behind us.

I was wrong. The ladder was disappearing through the hatch. The strig stared down at me.

"What are you doing?" I cried.

He said nothing. The hatch closed. The sound of something heavy being pushed over it scuffed at our ears.

"This is perfect," Ilyssa said calmly in her normal voice, all traces of the frightened chick gone now. She went to the furred boy and knelt before him.

"That hatch is the only way in or out. They want to *keep* us here," I said.

"I know." Ilyssa reached toward the boy, who sat up and watched her. "You'll be all right," she soothed. "I'm Miss Too. This is Kor. Do you remember us? We've come to help you."

"How can you say that?" I objected. "We're trapped. The Grays could…well, I don't know what they could do, but they must intend to do something with us or why would they shut us in?"

Stroking the boy's hand, Ilyssa told me, "They won't hurt us. Mellora will tell my father where I am. And because we're here, the Grays won't hurt this boy, either."

"You said your servant went off with Jass."

Ilyssa shook her head. "No, she's been following us. It's her job to make sure my sister and I are safe. Mellora's an orphan. She has no one but my family. She won't fail us."

"You *lied* to me?"

Indignant, Ilyssa insisted, "I didn't! I wasn't sure at first, but I saw Mellora when we were going down the ladder by my tree, and then again by the grounder thicket."

"Why didn't you say something to her—to me?"

"Because I thought you and I might get in trouble, and we have. I wanted her to keep her distance so she could bring help if we needed it. And I was right, wasn't I?"

I couldn't say that Ilyssa was wrong, but I didn't want to admit she was right. I felt tricked and left out of the plan, so I focused on the boy instead of Ilyssa.

In the cold blue light, he didn't look so good. The brown fur on his head was matted and some of the stringy fringe in front hung over his eyes. His face was dirty. The mask lay at his side, unused. His breathing was loud but steady.

Though he was much smaller than my brother, I guessed they were about the same age. He sat huddled with his arms around his knees, a strange pose, but then he didn't have wings to get in the way. He looked up at me, his dark eyes asking questions I couldn't answer. When the next fireball hit and the glyptos started bellowing again, he trembled.

Ilyssa patted his forearm and crooned to him. I gave her the cloak to put around the boy.

It was our fault that he was in this mess. If Ilyssa and I hadn't brought him to the Grays, he'd be…well, he'd be somewhere better than this. I understood now why she'd been so set on seeing him. I wanted him out of here and back where he belonged, wherever that was.

If only Ilyssa had trusted me—told me what she intended. She hadn't thought through this rescue. "What if no one comes because of the firefall?" I threw at her. "What if Mellora can't get back to your tree?"

Ilyssa turned away from the child and crossed her arms. "Then your friend will get help. *He* was following Mellora."

I had her now. "No way. Jass is on the fire squad, been volunteering for over a year. He's battling the blazes, not chasing after a pretty girl."

"You think Mellora is pretty?" Ilyssa inquired.

"Well…yeah, but that wouldn't keep Jass from fire squad duty."

Ilyssa finally looked worried. "Oh. I didn't know," she said in a small voice.

"Give me that glowrod. I'll check the walls. Maybe there's another way out."

I rolled the light in my hands curiously before prowling the edges of our prison, probing the stones, searching for any I could loosen with my fingers. If nothing else, I might be able to shout through a gap and get someone's attention.

By the walls, the noise outside was louder, and I realized this firefall had been going on too long. Usually, we just got a few blasts, the squad went out to smother fires and take the injured to a healer, and that was that.

Having the big animals crashing around was making things worse, I supposed, and this was odd, too. I couldn't remember glyptos running wild before. Their shells were hard as rock; tucked up inside, firefall couldn't hurt them. They weren't very smart, which was why we could keep them for food. What made them flee their corral?

I heard an alarm horn, then a grinding sound. Tilting my head, I listened to the crunching roll of the big stone wheels pulling out the overhead nets we use as a last defense against swarms. Every Midsummer's Day, the grounders opened the nets to inspect them, dozens of workers tugging on the leading edges while others raised support poles in a proud display of strength and teamwork.

It wasn't Midsummer. Had the firefall started an insect swarm? Coleos and myrmecs nested underground. Firefall shouldn't stir them up enough to begin a night march.

But if it wasn't a swarm, what was coming?

CHAPTER SIX

Escape

I'd just moved toward Ilyssa and the boy when stones behind me crashed in. I felt the shockwave as I jumped away from the collapsing wall.

"Look out!" Ilyssa cried.

I jigged sideways to avoid the spiked tail of a glypto slicing by me. The beast was half in and half out of the temple, part of its shell and one clawed foot wedged against the corner post. As it rocked to free itself, its deadly tail swung back and forth. I could see over the shell, so this was a smaller glypto, but it nearly filled the cramped space.

"Kor," I heard Jass' voice shout from outside. "You in there?"

"Yes! We're behind the glypto. It's stuck."

"No problem."

I thought we had a problem. Every time the glypto thrashed, the ceiling beams flexed and wood splinters rained down on us, but the beast suddenly stopped swaying to heave itself free of the wall. Lumbering off without a backward glance, the glypto gave way to Jass' grin.

"Hey," he said, climbing over the rubble. "Everybody all right?"

I coughed, then nodded. "How did you get it to leave?"

"It just needed a solid grip under its front foot. I shoved in a stone. Miss Too," he said formally, making a graceful half-bow. His eyes locked on the boy. "And this is it, the…the…?"

Ilyssa rose with a frown, dusting herself off irritably. "This is the furred boy. He's..." She looked down, extending a helping hand. "Well, we don't know his name." Tapping her own chest, she said to the boy, "Ilyssa."

He took her hand but said nothing.

"No time for chitchat," I pointed out. "Jass, what's going on out there?"

For once, he looked serious. "Tundran attack."

"WHAT?" Ilyssa and I gasped. Overhead, there were pounding footsteps and a scraping sound as the weight above the hatch moved.

Jass motioned us toward the hole in the wall. "Time to go."

Ilyssa draped her cloak around the boy and pulled him along. Then we were under the temple's overhang, too bewildered by the sights and sounds to take it in at once. People were shouting. I could make out flyers coming and going, silhouetted by moonlight against the grid of the nets. Every glowpot had been put out. I'd never seen the grove this way, and I was afraid.

Ilyssa whispered to Jass, "Mellora—Where is she?"

He pointed toward the grounder thicket where we could just make out the servant girl waving her hands at us. We ran to join her.

"I need to get to the knoll," Ilyssa said when we'd regrouped in a sorrel clump.

"Not the knoll, Mistress," Mellora told her gently. "That's where the raiders are trying to break through."

"My family!" Ilyssa cried.

"The hunters will protect them." Mellora's tone was reassuring, but she looked away when she said that.

"That's where we should go, then," Jass declared, "to fight."

I shook my head. "We should defend my mother and brother."

Jass looked thoughtful. "And my nieces and nephews."

"The little ones were sent to the stockade," Mellora told us, pointing toward the grounder fort. "I saw them flocking in after the first horn. There's a firefall shelter inside. The gates are sealed now."

It seemed we'd all forgotten about the fire. Gazing skyward again, I looked beyond the nets to make out a few streamers glimmering above. Wind had driven the storm higher. Cinders flickered down ominously.

"Look, let's all go to my tree," I said. "It's close, and there's more protection under the wide branches. We'll find a safe place for you girls, then Jass and I will go fight." I turned to leave the thicket but stopped. What was I thinking? We had the furred boy with us. He couldn't fly. Without wings, he was helpless as a nestling.

Ilyssa must have had the same thought. She said, "I'll get the wings."

The boy's strange wings had been taken inside the walls but kept under guard, Jass told me earlier. Though the guards would certainly be gone now, the area just inside the inner gate was bare of trees. Even with the nets in place, raiders could hover above, firing arrows or hurling spears.

"No, I'll go," I announced.

"The rest of you head for Kor's tree," Jass said decisively. Turning to me, he added, "I'll find the wings and see what's happening with the Tundrans. Stay in your home until I get there, and we'll figure out what to do next." Before I could object, he took off, and I had to admit to myself, at least, that he was much better in the air than I was, but I didn't like the admiring way Ilyssa gazed after him.

I carried the boy up to the roost, holding him with my arms wrapped around his chest. The flight was awkward and uncomfortable because his legs hung down. I felt discomfort for a different reason when I reached the roost and thought about taking Ilyssa to my home. It wasn't much compared to her villa.

When I lifted the drape away from the entrance, I found my mother strapping on her arrow quiver. "Kor! Oh, thank the gods you're safe." She hugged me and said, "I should be at the knoll, but there was no one to stay with the fledglings." Mom gestured toward Adom and the forager boy he'd been with this afternoon. They both looked ready to argue about needing protection. With a warning frown in their direction, my mother told me, "They missed the call to the stockade. You'll have to watch over them."

"Mother—" I began, but just then, Ilyssa, Mellora and the boy stepped in.

My mother's face shifted through a dozen expressions as she regarded the exalted Tropical champion, the wingless boy, and the servant. Her eyes rested longest on Mellora. "A *Tundran*, Kor? You've brought the enemy to our home?"

"I'm phasian stock," Mellora said emphatically. "We're grounders. Tundran hunters enslave us. After my mother was killed, a Tropical caravan found me." She looked at Ilyssa. "The Toos took me in. I'm grateful for my life here."

My mother wasn't convinced. Her eyes narrowed. "You could be a spy."

"I'd rather *die* than serve Tundran hunters," Mellora declared.

After blowing out her cheeks with a gusty sigh, Mom ran a hand through her crown feathers. She said to me, "The raiders could attack our Hunters' Ring next."

"Jass and I intend to fight."

"This raid will turn into a siege. The Tundrans can't get through our nets, and they can't fight by day, when they'd be easy targets for our arrows. They'll have to set up camp nearby. There, they'll be vulnerable.

Go to the Shore folk and ask them for weapons and warriors. If they fail us, get Mountaineer hunters or even the Chiros."

"Why would Chiros help us?" I asked.

"They owe us a debt. We saved them from a day raid some years back. Here...." My mother went to the baskets where we keep things we don't use every day. She lifted one from the back and blew away the dust. Reaching inside, she handed me a carved clay circle on a neck string. "Give them this to jog their memories."

"Chiros are beasts," Ilyssa protested.

My mother shook her head. "They're different, but they're not beasts. In fact," she looked closely at the furred boy, "they're not so much stranger than this one. What are you planning to do with him?"

"The Grays want him dead," Ilyssa said. "We freed him so he could rejoin his people, but we don't know where they are."

"Perhaps you'll find them along the way." Mother turned to the fledglings. "Gather warm wraps, bedding, and food. Prepare to leave."

The forager boy said, "We want to stay here to help."

Mother said firmly, "You will help the older wings recruit allies, Lucan. Begin by packing supplies."

I stood watching my mother, marveling at the change in her. Ordinarily, she wasn't one to take charge. She was a hunter, and a good one, I'd heard, but she always flew with the cast. I'd never thought of her fighting Tundrans. Her brown plumage was lightening with age. I said, "I'm afraid for you."

"Your father will guard my wings, and I'll guard his."

Still troubled, my thoughts must have shown on my face, for Mother hugged me again and then held both my hands, saying, "Now this is what you must do...."

Half an hour later, we'd made our way to the south bank of the stream that ran through the deep ravine of our grove. This was our fresh water supply, a torrent in the spring, but sluggish during this moon. The stream passed through a tunnel in the walls to fall from the cliff to the seashore below.

Jass had brought the furred boy's wings, but the boy refused to wear them. He tapped on one side and babbled heatedly. Nobody understood what he meant until Ilyssa remarked, "The wings need sunlight so they can fly. He keeps pointing to a light sensor."

"A what?"

"A sensor—here." Ilyssa turned the wings so I could see the back. "This makes them work."

I gaped at her. "How do you know that?"

She rubbed her forehead and said, "I just do. Anyway, it's night now, so they have to be carried, but water won't hurt them."

"You sure this is the place?" Jass interrupted.

"Yes." Chewing on a lip, I looked toward the stone grating blocking the tunnel. Past that obstacle, we might not have room enough inside the tunnel to avoid soaking our wings, making them useless for flight. It would be death to jump from the cliff.

I looked at the netting above our heads. The edges were anchored to lines between rollers on the outer wall. Our nets were made with many layers of braided rhino hide, too tough even for firestone blades. We hadn't any knives, and besides, a cut in the web would create a hole for Tundrans to use. We couldn't leave Sea Grove through the net.

"There *has* to be a way out," Adom insisted, "or Mother wouldn't have sent us here."

Lucan had been studying the tunnel. "There's a stone in the wall that looks different from the rest. If we pull it out…." He tugged on the stone.

"It lifts the grating!"

We watched the grating rise. It stayed up until Lucan shoved the stone back into place. The grating went down slowly enough for a person to slip through before the opening shut.

"That stone's too far away from the tunnel for anyone inside to reach. Tundrans can't get in." In her excitement, Ilyssa spoke too loudly. I waved my hands at her. We didn't want any raiders flying overhead to hear us.

She whispered when she explained, "It'll be tricky to fit through the tunnel, but if we're careful to hold our wings high, we'll be fine. Then all we have to do is fly down to the Shores' camp."

"Easy for you to say," I grumbled. "You'll fit the tunnel with room to spare."

"True," she agreed, "and so will the fledglings, but I'll spot their descent anyway. You *can* fly?" After checking for nods from Adom and Lucan, she added, "Then, well, um…"

"Him," Lucan cut in, pointing at Jass. "He goes through and catches the false wings floated down the stream by Adom's brother. Adom's brother—"

"Kor," I informed him. "And that's Jass, Ilyssa—er, Miss Too—and Mellora. We'll call the stranger…"

"Chipmunk," Jass suggested, "'cause he's small and furry."

"Oh, now, I don't think—" Ilyssa began.

"Chip," I said. "We can find a better name later. For now, that'll do."

Lucan nodded, and went on with his strategy. "After Kor goes through, he waits to ferry Chip to the ground. The supply bag is oiled outside and has a layer of fish bladder to keep things dry; it will float. You, Miss, catch the bag pushed through by your servant. She fixes the grating and leaves before it closes. That's it."

Everyone stared at him. Lucan shrugged. "Seems obvious."

"We're really going to do this?" I asked, rubbing the back of my neck. "No one else thinks this is crazy?"

Adom threw out his hands. "Do you have a better idea?"

I exhaled heavily. Jass pulled on the stone in the wall. The grating creaked open.

Wading into the stream, Ilyssa flinched when the cold water soaked her legs. I realized then that our wet shin feathers wouldn't steady our flights, so I prayed silently for still air along the cliff face. My prayer was pointless: It's always windy by the sea.

Ilyssa stumbled. I was afraid she'd be drenched and unable to fly, but she found her balance and slogged into the tunnel, bending low to keep her wings high and dry. I held my breath when she disappeared, but after we waited for a time and heard nothing from her, Adom followed, and then Lucan went through. Jass had to get down on hands and knees to enter the tunnel, swearing vigorously as the icy stream soaked through the front of his clothes. When he'd been gone for what I thought would be long enough, I shoved Chip's wings into the water and watched them float away.

It was my turn to brave the waterfall.

CHAPTER SEVEN

Death

"Good luck," Mellora whispered as she took Ilyssa's cape from Chip and added it to the supply sack. She waved cheerily. Chip watched without emotion.

"Thanks," I muttered over my shoulder. I moved into the stream.

Yeow! I knew why Jass had been so foul about the cold water. It was bone chilling. In the tunnel...well, I hate closed-in spaces. They make me feel like I can't breathe. I was so relieved to get out of that place that I didn't worry much about the waterfall edge. As my wings filled out, I swayed a bit, but not too bad: I was flying fine.

For an instant, I relived the thrill of my flight with Jass over the sea by the knoll. Had that been only hours ago?

Below, on the narrow, rocky beach between cliff and waves, I spotted Ilyssa and the others. I'd expected them to go around the cliff to the cove where the Shores usually camp, but I remembered Ilyssa was supposed to come back for our traveling gear. It was better for everyone to stay together. All right, then: The plan was going smoothly. I turned to wait for Chip.

He was already at the end of the tunnel, arms and legs spread wide, clinging to the opening like a nid on its web. I couldn't go right up against the cliff face to get him because the same strong wind that made it easy to lift off from the edge made it dangerous to get too near. If I smashed into the rock and broke a wing, we'd both fall, but if Mellora sent through the supplies and the bag knocked Chip over the edge, I wouldn't be there to catch him.

Gritting my teeth, I flew as close as I dared, then shouted at him to let go and to jump away from the edge. Of course, he had no idea what I was saying, but I don't think he'd have done what I wanted even if he understood. He was scared, so scared his eyes weren't focusing on me. They were staring at the rocks below.

Scat! What could I do? Any minute now, that bag was going to come through.

From the corner of my eye, I saw a flash of white and knew it was Ilyssa. No one else flies like she does, holding her head low so the air streams past her crown to fill her wings, wings that blur with their speed. She was heading straight for Chip to rescue him because she didn't trust me.

I'm not proud of what came next. I couldn't let her show me up that way, but just as I feared, the wind kept forcing me toward the cliffs so I had to backwing away. I kept trying, flapping my wings while my body swung wildly back and forth, blocking Ilyssa from edging past me to do the job I was failing at.

She cried, "Kor! Get out of the way. Give me room."

"NO!" I roared.

Ilyssa did something then that was so reckless, I couldn't believe my eyes. Rising several body lengths above me, she snapped her wings back, throwing herself at the cliff. She hit hard, then slid, scraping her hands until her fingers seized on tiny lumps in the rock and her right foot wedged into a cleft no wider than my fist. Her left wing was now deep in the waterfall spray, getting wetter by the second, but she reached an arm to the boy and he took it. She held his eyes, nodded at him, and he leapt into her grasp just as she fell away from the cliff.

I heard a scream ring through the tunnel.

An enormous, dark flyer drifted over the walls above the net. Each of his wings was longer than both of mine. His face and arms were painted skeleton white; his bare chest, blood red. From waist to knees he wore plated rhino hide. Dense shin feathers overlapped firestone talons and jagged heel spurs. Though his passage overhead must have taken only seconds, it seemed like minutes before the monster swept by.

He'd seen everything below as he passed. He wheeled, slowly, so slowly. One brawny arm shot out and he pointed at Ilyssa.

She shrieked. Who could blame her? Death itself had singled her out. Still, the girl who'd braved the cliffs now defied death again, heading straight out to sea.

Jass shot up from the shore. The monster turned his head briefly, then ignored him. The death head profile watched the heavily burdened girl with the sodden left wing who was vainly streaking over the waves. She looked so small.

There's a call hunters make. My parents call it the Kill Scree because the sound freezes prey in its tracks. It's a call to submission, an announcement as final as fate. The Tundran monster made this call, and I hope I never hear its like again.

Ilyssa was flying toward an island, just a tiny spit of land, but there were trees—*cover*. She wouldn't make it in time. The Tundran languidly lifted his wings, beat once, and soared effortlessly after her. Nothing could stop him.

I tried to shout, but my voice broke. My body took over from my horror-numbed mind. I was flying faster than I'd ever imagined I could, seeing everything as if it were a dream unfolding, something unreal.

I tore on, having no idea where my strength and speed were coming from. All my attention was fixed on the Tundran. I noticed tiny details about him—how his primaries curved on the down stroke, how he held his knees slightly below his brutal feet. One covert feather was loose. Curious.

The world narrowed. I saw only the Tundran's outline. This grew larger and larger as I closed the gap between us. I wondered what I would do when I caught him.

Instinctively, I spread my wings out full and pulled hard, shooting upward until I was high above the Tundran. I could see Ilyssa. Her wing beats were no longer steady, but ragged and desperate.

For a moment, I felt helpless, confused. Then everything changed.

All the questions were gone. Without thinking about it, I folded my wings, and dropped. I hadn't lost control; I knew exactly what I was doing.

The Tundran never saw it coming. He didn't know that all the weight of my body, all the force of my will and ancestry would surge through two inches of heel to crush the smallest bones in his neck. He gave one absurd, little squawk, his great wings arced up nearly encircling me, and then he fell.

The body didn't sink. It floated face down, wings open, like a raft. Before I followed Ilyssa to the island, I rested on it.

I found her on a pebbly beach, sitting on a rock, head in hands, sobbing. Chip stood beside her, clumsily stroking her shoulder. She looked at me—a long look of gratitude and reproach—then she went back to her crying.

When the others joined us, I accepted Jass' excited pounding and Mellora's praise. Adom dubbed me "Kor, Monster Slayer," and kept listing all the people he wanted to tell about this. Lucan regarded me with something like fear in his eyes.

I slipped away. I'd just made my first kill. I needed to jump up and down. I needed to bellow my victory to the skies. I needed to throw up.

"The Shore folk are gone," Adom reported after I returned. "Their campsite was abandoned. Where did they go?"

That was a good question but one that would have to wait until morning. For now, we needed warmth and cover. We were less than a mile offshore. Another Tundran hunter, or even a cast of them, could appear at any time.

Mellora was applying seaweed to Ilyssa's raw palms. Ilyssa waved her away, saying, "I saw glowpots on this island."

"Are you sure?" Lucan asked. He pursed his lips and shivered.

"Yes," Ilyssa said flatly. "Mellora, what happened to the supplies?"

"I have the bag. I carried it while I flew." The servant girl made this remark with just the faintest hint of a smirk. The rest of us don't expect grounders to be skilled flyers; maybe we underestimate them. They're not fast, but some do migrate long distances, and they're very strong.

Mellora dipped into the bag. She withdrew her hand, wrinkling her nose. "Moisture seeped in. I hope the food isn't spoiled."

"Is there anything dry to wear?" Ilyssa asked, wrapping her arms around herself. "I'm freezing." To everyone's surprise, Chip slid inside her wings to embrace her, and she leaned her cheek wearily against his furry head.

Mellora smiled. "I'll look, Miss."

She found the cloak, which had been packed last and so was dry. After wrapping this around Ilyssa, Mellora dispensed raccoon-skin wraps all around. She didn't take one for herself.

"What about you?" Lucan wondered, as he pulled the edges of his cape tighter.

"I will not be cold, though I will be glad for some leggings."

Jass looked wistful as Mellora's luxurious shin feathers disappeared inside the leather breeches she pulled on. He said, "We should move into the trees."

"Yes," Mellora agreed. "Tundran hunters will be searching for that chieftain."

"Chieftain?" I asked.

"Mmm. That one you downed was no ordinary Tundran. He was important, and will be missed. Let us ask that watcher, there, for sanctuary." After this astonishing statement, Mellora took herself over to a clump of weeds. "On behalf of my mistress and her escort, I beg shelter for the night," she said.

Weeds rose up, unfurling like a fern, to become a short, thin man under a cloak. His garment had been crafted of sea grass and driftwood tied onto fine netting. I marveled at the disguise of the watcher, and vowed to remember it.

The man was old. He said in a raspy voice, "Why have you come here?"

Ilyssa stepped forward. "As my servant said, to seek sanctuary and to search out the Shores who camped in the cove. Are you one of those? We ask your help for Sea Grove in fighting the Tundran raiders."

"That one..." he pointed to Chip, "is strange. What weapon does he carry?"

"No weapon. Those are his wings, which he removes at night."

The man fingered his chin, scrutinizing Chip and then the rest of us. "You are young to speak for your people," he said to Ilyssa.

"We are, and yet that is our mission. Will you help us?"

"I do not decide such things. Come. You must address the Mothers."

He guided us along a twisting, shell-strewn path that led up the central rise of the narrow island. Under fragrant firs, I felt my spirits lift. We were well hidden here: No Tundran would take us by surprise.

We stopped on the windward edge of the island, facing open water. It seemed an odd place for a camp, but we discovered that's what it was when Shores began to emerge from sealskin lean-tos covered with branches and grass. The ground had been dug away beneath, making sleeping spaces. Suddenly, I felt very tired.

The watcher brought three elderly women to us, introducing them as the Mothers, leaders of this flock. Larger than the man, their plumage was mottled brown and white. Their clothing was made of sea animal hide laced at the sides. Ilyssa began to tell them our story, but they hushed her in a kind but firm way, insisting that we eat our fill of fish chowder or seaweed soup, then stay in one of their ground nests until morning.

Ilyssa and Mellora settled in first, with Chip beside them. I had never slept outside my own trees. I thought I would be restless, caught up in the newness of sounds and smells, fearful for my people or plagued by memories of the Tundran chieftain, but sleep took me the instant I lay down between Adom and Jass.

And so we passed our first night away from our grove among the Shores.

CHAPTER EIGHT

Shores

I woke with my heart pounding. Something was wrong. There was a jumble of bodies around me—clothing and feathers and skin. Where was I?

Squinting, I held up a hand against the glare. As memory flooded back, I saw Ilyssa gripping the flap to the lean-to, searching with her eyes for a spot inside the ground nest where we'd slept. I heaved Jass' foot off my shin and elbowed Adom over a bit, bending my legs to make room for her.

"You went out?"

"Mmm. I talked with one of the Mothers. Her name is Lydia."

I sat forward. "What did Lydia say?"

Ilyssa shrugged. "We have to go."

"*Go*? Why?"

"Wake the others," she said briskly, tapping Chip's shoulder. "They might as well hear this, too."

The Shores couldn't promise fighters or weapons for our grove. "They have none," Ilyssa reported. "Shores don't believe in defending territory. They'd rather move than lose any of their flock."

"Cowards," Adom muttered.

"No, they're not. Lydia said they think fighting is wrong, so they're always prepared to break camp. They don't keep anything they can't carry with them. As long as they're together by the sea, they have all they need."

Jass asked, "What about those spears they use for fishing? Couldn't those be weapons?"

Ilyssa shook her head. "The tridents are too heavy to throw. When I mentioned them to Lydia, she said catching fish in the water wasn't the same as catching men in the air."

I pictured the chieftain I'd left floating face down. "Did she know anything about what's happening in the grove?"

"Yes. She sent scouts to see how our people are doing. The nets are holding, thank the gods."

"Scouts? Wasn't that risky?" Lucan wondered.

"The Shores aren't cowards," Ilyssa insisted. "Lydia told me her people would get us to Stillwaters, who can lead us to Mountaineers. If the Mountaineer hunters come to fight with us, the Shores will help by spying, carrying messages, making traps or ambush places—anything they can do by moving around unseen."

I nodded, thinking about the disguised watcher last night and the hidden camp we were in. "All right, but how do we leave here without the Tundrans attacking us?"

"Lydia has a plan."

The little island lay bathed in morning fog. This weather was key to our escape, Lydia told us, while we hurriedly ate fish (most of us) or apples and grapes (Ilyssa and Mellora). "Just now, the fog is heavy. Tundrans will not fly—too much moisture for the wings—and the mist will conceal your departure."

"We'll have the same problem with our feathers," I pointed out.

"You will have the boats," Lydia said.

I blinked, certain this was a bad idea. The Shores made tiny, one- or two-person fishing boats covered with sealskin. Their fish catchers sat deep inside, below the waterline. I'd always thought those contraptions looked dangerous. What if a big wave came along? I didn't want to drown.

"You will not drown," Lydia soothed as though she heard my thoughts.

I flinched, and she chuckled. "You are not the first to distrust the sealboats. You will see how well they work. We have yet to lose any of our flock."

We're not Shores, I thought bleakly, but I didn't say that aloud. Instead, I reminded her, "We don't know how to handle the boats."

"Thomis will be your teacher and guide."

Thomis turned out to be the watcher from last night. Now I was really worried: He was an old man.

"Putting a sealboat together is easy," Thomis assured us as he laid sewn skins on the beach. Removing long, wooden pieces from a sack, he matched notches, then placed smaller, curved upright ribs along the sides. Gripping each half of the frame in turn, he slid these into a skin and fastened them together. Two flexible slats bowed out to form the round cockpit rim. After checking the fit everywhere and tightening some strapping around horn, Thomis was done. "There, now. That's all there's to it. Got that?"

Lucan said, "Yes. It's not too hard."

Thomis beamed at him. "All right. By the time you're in your spraycoats, I'll have the other boats ready for you."

"These look like ladies' gowns," Adom complained. He revolved stiffly in place with his arms held out. The sealskin garment had a hood and a wide skirt that looked decidedly girly. It felt confining and heavy,

I discovered, when it was my turn to put one on.

Looking at me, Jass broke out laughing. Mellora shushed him, saying, "Keep your voice low. Let's not tell *every* Tundran hunter in the area where we are."

Subdued, Jass was the first to have his spraycoat laced into the boat he would share with Lucan. He'd made a strong pitch for traveling with Mellora, but she offered to take charge of our gear, including Chip's wings. Though Jass pretended to be crushed by her rejection, I knew he was already thinking of how to improve her opinion of him. Jass couldn't resist a challenge.

I was teamed with Adom; Ilyssa, with Chip. This was fine; I needed to look out for my brother, and I wasn't happy with Ilyssa. She'd said nothing to me about yesterday though I saved her life. She should be grateful. *Girls...* Anyway, Thomis had paired older and younger wings, which was probably the best way to go after all.

We said our thanks and goodbyes to Lydia, waved to the Shores who'd been peeking at us from their hidden nests, and practiced paddling a while before we headed off.

After we left the island, the plan was for us to stay in open water until we were far enough from Sea Grove to evade the Tundran raiders. Making for a bay formed by the mouth of a large river, we would leave Thomis there with the boats and fly on to a Stillwater settlement.

We couldn't get back to land fast enough to suit me. The water was rough from last night's firestorm; the waves were high. I hoped the little boats would stay upright and that the coats we wore would really keep us dry.

"They'll hold out the water even if you roll," Thomis explained while describing how to right ourselves in an overturned boat. *Roll?* I didn't want to roll. I didn't want to be tied in by laces, either. I felt trapped. I wanted out of the boat, out of the sea, out—

"Kor?" Ilyssa called. "Are you all right?" Like everything else Ilyssa did, handling her boat with ease seemed to come naturally. Chip matched her strokes exactly.

"I'm fine," I lied, pulling an extra-hard stroke. That move flung water in Adom's face and earned me a whack from his paddle, but we'd sped ahead of Ilyssa to a position between Jass and Thomis.

"Stay in the fog," Thomis commanded, "and be silent."

By the time the fog lifted, we were far from home. The land here was lower than around our grove. Rolling hills bright with colorful trees sloped down to wave-cut sandbanks. Rings of frothy, white surf lapped at pillars of sea rock. Though it was a pleasant area, I missed the tall trees and proud cliffs of home; they were majestic, grand. I decided that the Shores were wrong: Some land was worth fighting for.

We passed two Shore folk camps, and I wondered why they hadn't moved on to avoid the Tundrans. I asked Thomis about that.

"Tundrans don't seek us," he told me. "Our possessions are few, just the skins, tools and boats. We don't make good slaves because we die if we're away from the sea too long."

"So why did your flock move?"

"Since they couldn't get into your grove, the Tundran raiders might have turned on us for spite," Thomis reasoned. "We didn't want to take that chance, so—Look there."

My eyes followed his pointing paddle. A gnarled, gray sea beast rose half out of the waves to throw itself at the sky, then fell back to slap the water. It was enormous. The surge it created made our boats bob like seeds on a fast-moving stream. I was afraid the monster would swim beneath my boat and fling Adom and me into the air.

Seeing my reaction, Thomis grinned. He said, "The miwak never harm us. From below, we may resemble their calves." His voice suddenly took on a sharp note. "Fledgling! Do not lean so far to the side."

Thomis was talking to Adom. I swiveled my head as best I could in the stiff hood, only to find Adom retching into the water. When he finished, he washed his mouth with seawater and looked completely miserable. I grinned at him, trying to pluck up his spirits, wishing I could do more. We hunters were not meant for the sea.

Neither, it turned out, was Mellora. She was having trouble controlling her boat. Strong as she was, she paddled alone with a heavy load. The current kept pushing her toward the beach, and she lagged behind. A considerable distance now separated her from the rest of us.

"Girl! Steer clear of that shore," Thomis called.

"I'm trying!" Mellora yelled.

Thomis turned and stroked toward her, barking more instructions. "Head around those rocks—around them into the bay, you hear?"

Whether Mellora heard him or not didn't matter. Paddling hard, she was still washing closer to rocky mudflats below a sandbank riddled with dark blots.

One of the blots moved.

Ilyssa screamed. That's all you can do when a coleo appears—see it and cry out. They move too fast to do anything else.

An orange-brown blur whizzed from its burrow to the rocks, leaping for Mellora's head with its sickle-shaped pincers wide. From the corner of my eye, I could see more of its hairy, six-legged companions spilling out of holes and scrambling down the bank.

The gods must have been with us because one of them sent a wave that saved Mellora's life. Her boat, unbalanced by the huge insect poised on one side and the wave hitting opposite, rolled over. The coleo went under, then it surfaced, spindly forelegs groping frantically for land.

Thomis had already freed himself from his boat and jumped to the rocks, waving his paddle. The coleos who'd been after Mellora studied the old man with their great, glossy brown eyes, lifted their bristling antennae, and rushed him.

They first one's jaws crunched down on Thomis' paddle. Confused by this tasteless morsel, the coleo twisted left and right, unwilling to chew the splinters or to spit them out. That beast's thrashing blocked the others from advancing, except for a small one that slipped by to tear into the coat Thomis threw at it as he dove into the water. In seconds, he reached Mellora's overturned craft and yanked it away from the coleo-covered rocks.

Jass yelled and slapped his paddle on the water. The hungry coleos focused on this new target. Lucan had his coat front loose and slashed with a firestone knife at the laces keeping Jass tied to the boat. Wrenching off his spraycoat, Jass hurled it toward the rocks before standing in his cockpit, wobbling wildly. Lucan yelped in alarm, then plunged his paddle deep into the water to steady the boat until Jass lifted off.

Using himself as bait, Jass went into a teasing, taunting air dance just above the coleos. The group closest to him stood on their hindmost legs, straining to reach up and grab him.

Ilyssa paddled in as close as she dared, taking up the cry Jass and Lucan began, slapping the water while shouting insults. When Chip chimed in with that weird, rumbling voice of his, I don't know who was more surprised, the coleos or the rest of us.

I was struggling against my laces, but they wouldn't give. Without a knife, I couldn't get free. Adom was trying vainly to untie himself. Fools that we were, we both stopped paddling at the same time, letting the waves push us so close to the coleos that we could count the coarse, white hairs on the brutes' dark heads. We back-paddled like mad to escape jaws clicking with eagerness to eat us.

Thomis had righted Mellora's boat. The servant girl lay with her head hanging down, spewing seawater from her mouth. Thomis gripped a boat strap with one hand, swimming against the waves to tow the craft into deeper water.

I let out the breath I didn't know I'd been holding, but it wasn't over yet. The coleos were too excited to give up. A big one climbed over two others and clamped onto Jass' leg.

Jass pulled hard with his wings, lifting himself and the coleo. The coleo hung suspended from Jass until it whacked into the sandbank where another coleo lunged from its burrow and clipped off the first one's head. As the body fell, Jass shot up to a perch on a dead tree atop the sandbank. He shook off the still-attached coleo head. Shuddering, he looked down at his left leg. The shin feathers had been cropped close to the skin. That was all. No blood. No wound.

I whooped. Jass wasn't crippled. Mellora hadn't drowned. No one was eaten. Around me, everyone howled, releasing fear and joy, even Mellora, who'd recovered enough to shout feebly and pound her fist on the drenched sealboat deck.

Thomis waved at Lucan, who stroked over to him. Tying Mellora's boat to Lucan's, the old man pulled himself into Jass' empty cockpit as nimbly as if he were a fledgling. He shook out his wings and took up Jass' paddle.

We reclaimed Thomis' boat and left the infested rocks behind to enter a wide bay. On a flat, open sandbar with a clear view of everything around us, we stopped to rest and to eat. The river leading to the Stillwaters' settlement lay ahead.

It was nearly time for Thomis to leave us. I would be sorry to see the old man go.

CHAPTER NINE

Stillwaters

It was late afternoon before we reached the Stillwaters' crannogs, a group of fenced islands built on posts sunk into a marshy lake. Some islands held buildings while others looked like giant cages. A wide, round hall with a thatched roof filled the largest island, which was connected to dry ground by a bridge.

Coleos crawled all over the place. There wasn't a person in sight.

These coleos were smaller than the ones that attacked us by the sea. They were only half a man's height and had grooved, blue backs, red foreparts and dull brown eyes. From the air, they looked almost silly as they wandered around, waggling their antennae at everything in a dopey sort of way. They might have been lost glyptos.

But glyptos didn't eat people. Had these coleos killed the Stillwaters? If we went closer, would we find only gory bits of the folk who'd built the settlement?

We circled overhead but had to land somewhere soon. Chip's wings were losing strength. As the skies darkened with clouds, he'd flown lower and lower until he'd leveled out just above the river. There had been rapids in places, the churning waters driving against the run of green-and-red fish trying to swim upstream. When we finally spotted the Stillwater village, I felt relief, but now I wasn't sure what to do.

I'd grown used to Chip and his wings during the time we spent flying together. It's interesting how something so strange can seem normal if you give up on thinking it's impossible. Chip's wings were like that. They didn't move like ours did but stayed in the same position as air rushed through them, lifting Chip somehow.

Back when we stopped for lunch on the sandbar, he'd taken his wings out of Mellora's sealboat, inspected them, turned them over so their back faced the sky, and then sat down to eat with the rest of us. He tried both the dried meat and the nuts my mother packed, then he sampled clams Thomis dug for his own meal.

Lucan had been equally eager for any sort of food. After Jass teased him about his odd eating habits, Lucan struck up a defensive friendship with Chip.

Chip babbled at Lucan for a while, and Lucan tried to repeat the sounds. His attempts made both of them laugh. Though Chip's laughter sounded like he was standing at the bottom of a ravine, it sparked an idea in Lucan. "I think he's speaking our language," he explained excitedly to Adom. "His words are just so slow and deep they're hard to make out."

Intrigued by this notion, Ilyssa moved nearer the fledglings to listen. Mellora was still recovering from her ordeal, so she rested while Jass and I carried the boats to the top of a rise where Thomis thought they'd be safe until he returned with other Shores.

He gave us one of the fine nets his people used to hide themselves. "Might come in handy if you run into trouble. Coat it with mud, then stick on whatever's on the ground around you." Thomis told us to follow the river, and when it forked, to take the left fork. "Soon after that, you'll come to the Stillwaters' crannogs."

"I really know nothing about Stillwaters," I admitted. "The only ones I've seen were entertainers—musicians, dancers, actors—brought to our grove by Tropical caravans. How can they help us?"

"These will be large people with black-and-white crowns and gray-brown wings," Thomis said. "Each year, they travel to and from the Tropical zone, seeing all along the way. They will know where Mountaineers can be found. I just hope the Stillwaters haven't left for their wintering ground."

Looking down now on the Stillwaters' overrun settlement, I was hoping they *had* gone rather than been eaten by coleos, even though that would be a setback for us. I'd almost convinced myself they'd left when I saw a young female such as Thomis described—large, dark headed with white side patches and brownish wings—step out from the hall on the main island, walk calmly among the coleos, and raise both hands to signal us. She flew up to our level, called a greeting, and motioned us to one of the smaller islands where we landed on a platform above a cage.

"Gods' wings, I'm glad to see you!" she said, clapping Jass on the shoulder so heartily he stumbled against Adom. She raised her fist in greeting. "I'm Chaya—Chaya Anser."

I was prepared for a big person, but this massive girl towered over us. I felt like a nestling compared to her, and yet she had a young face. Wearing strips of leather and an apron made of marsh reeds, Chaya Anser was large in all her proportions, a fact that brought a wry smile to her lips when she noticed Jass ogling her. Looped around her left arm, she had bangles of rope with colored patches on them. Slipping these off, she shoved the lot at Jass, saying, "Here, Bold Eyes, take a band and pass the rest around."

"Why are you giving us bracelets?" I asked. "What's happened here?"

"Those are wrangler bands. Our catch of coleos escaped," the girl said. "Without them, we'll starve. That's why we recruited you."

Adom made a terrible face, then blurted out, "You *eat* coleos?"

"Not these!" Chaya sputtered. "We train racing coleos—jewel boxes—for the Winter Games." She added with obvious pride, "Ours have been grand champions for the last two seasons."

"The Winter Games in Ladana? I know about those," Ilyssa said. "My mother swears my father organizes winter caravans to the empire's capital just so he can be in the great city to bet on the Games." Ilyssa rolled her eyes. "Mother says he gambles too much."

"Who's your father?" Chaya asked.

"Aurelius Too."

"Go on! You're Honorable Too's daughter? He always bets on our racers and wins." Chaya chuckled in disbelief. "And he sent *you* to wrangle coleos?"

Ilyssa looked shocked. "I'm afraid there's been some mistake. We came to ask for your help. Sea Grove is under attack. A flock of Shores said you Stillwaters could point us toward Mountaineer warriors who would help us fight the Tundrans."

Chaya did a double take. "Our help? *We* need *your* help." She surveyed our group while we told her our names. "Woodlanders, one Tundran, one Tropical. What are you?" she asked Chip.

Lucan answered, "He's our friend. We're taking him home."

"To where?" Chaya strode around Chip, scrutinizing him and his strapped-on wings. She reached to touch his furry head, but changed her mind and pulled back her hand. With a resigned shrug, she returned her attention to Ilyssa. "You're small for this work, but with Brant away, I need all the wings I can get."

"Brant?" Jass asked.

"My mate. He flew north yesterday to find wranglers. I thought he'd sent you."

I raised an eyebrow. Chaya wasn't much older than we were. *Young,* I thought, *to have a mate.* I had a lot to learn about Stillwaters.

Chaya peered anxiously at the sky. "Brant should have been back by now."

There was an uncomfortable silence until Lucan suggested, "If he went looking for help from Sea Grove, he'll be blocked by the Tundran attack. He'll have to go elsewhere, and that'll take more time."

Nodding thoughtfully, Chaya said, "You're right. I'm sorry about your grove, but I don't know how to fight Tundrans. They won't attack us—why should they? This marsh freezes over in winter, so if they want it, they can have it. Our coleos?" She snorted. "They wouldn't know the first thing about tending them. If they stole the racing jewels, they'd kill them and get nothing."

"Couldn't they capture you to make you work for them?" Adom asked.

"Not if they wanted to stay healthy. Living where we do, we have to understand insect venoms. Would you want a person who knows a lot about poison as *your* slave?"

While we mulled over that thought, Chaya went on, "The rest of my people have gone to Ladana to get choice wintering ground while it's still available, but Brant and I waited until the really big jewels hatched. We're on our own."

"How many coleos are you missing?" I asked. "What do they look like?"

"Four. Jewel boxes are green with blue rosettes on their wing covers. They're still in the marsh—plenty of food here—but they hide after dark, and it takes a team to catch one, so...." She counted us. "There are enough for the job. We'll have to work fast while there's light enough to see."

"What about those red coleos crawling all over the place?" Lucan asked.

"Those are gassers, and they only eat other insects. If you look below us, you'll see two pens, one inside the other. We keep gassers in the outer ring and the jewels inside. The jewels don't get near the gassers because they spray boiling fluid when they're touched, but yesterday, the jewels chewed through a fence section, then shoved it aside as they left, blocking the gassers until they got out, too." Chaya frowned and shook her head. "I fixed the holes in the pen today. Just ignore the loose gassers—oh, but don't touch them. If you do, they'll scald you."

"I'm not sure..." Mellora began with a protective glance toward Ilyssa.

"What do we do first?" Jass wanted to know.

I sighed as Ilyssa asked Chaya, "If we help you find your coleos today, you'll direct us to Mountaineers first thing tomorrow morning?"

"Deal."

The Great Coleo Roundup started with Chaya giving us instructions. "Open the green pouches on the bands I gave you," she told Jass and me, "and close the others. You won't need them. Those pouches are for other types of insects."

I prodded the green flap on my band with a fingertip. Inside, I found a smear of what looked like fat. It smelled vaguely fishy. "You're sure these gadgets will keep the coleos from eating us?"

The Stillwater girl grinned. "They won't eat you, but they might fall in love with you. That's female jewel scent—works like a love potion. My Brant makes the bands," Chaya added proudly. "Everyone else should open their red pouches. That'll trick the jewels into thinking you're a gasser."

"Won't the gassers come after us?"

"No. That's their warning scent."

I grimaced and stared at my wrist, then shook it uneasily. Jass and I were to be what Chaya called "lures". What she meant, of course, was bait. That didn't bother Jass since he'd already been coleo bait this morning, but I had to get used to the idea.

As a love-struck jewel box yearned for Jass or me, Chaya was to rope its head, then Adom and Lucan would prod it with poles until it neared the outer pen, where the other bait person would wave scent at it from the closed inner cage. The coleo would step into the outer ring and be trapped. Mellora had the job of handling the cage door, while Ilyssa flew overhead, looking for more coleos. Chip would stand watch on the pen platform.

It was a plan. I hoped it would work.

No sooner had I flown by a pile of fallen leaves than a bright green head popped up, waving its antennae. I shot higher instantly—the thing was bigger by half than the orange-brown ones by the sea—and Chaya flung her rope from behind it to lasso the jewel's head. Adom and Lucan nudged it toward Jass in the cage. The coleo scrambled forward. Chaya released her rope, and Mellora shut the cage door. Success!

It took longer to find the next jewel, but we caught it, and a third one, as easily as the first. With just one more coleo to go, I started thinking about my empty stomach and when we'd get to eat. It seemed like a long, long time since lunch.

Chip bellowed as a big bubble popped up from the water next to the pen. What I'd taken for a dark leaf became the head and thick, bent pincer legs of something so huge that it rose to equal my pitch above the swamp. Two stony eyes separated by what looked like a beak stared at me.

The beak struck me in the chest. I felt a stab of hot agony shoot through me, and then I felt nothing.

When I woke, I thought Tundran hunters were tearing into my head with firestone talons. I was alive, but that wasn't good news.

Groaning, I forced one eyelid open just long enough to see I lay inside a high, domed structure. From the size, it had to be the big hall. My head was resting against something soft and warm. I couldn't feel the rest of my body. Panicked, I tried to shout, but the sound that came out was a garbled croak.

"He's awake," I heard Ilyssa call from above my head. "Chaya, come here!"

I'd have flinched from the noise if I could have moved, but nothing below my throat worked, and my throat wasn't working well. Swallowing was a struggle.

The big girl's face swam into view. She touched my forehead and peered into my eyes. Finally, she smiled at me. "Don't worry. The weakness will pass. You just need more of this."

She did something to my chest that I couldn't feel. While she was doing that, I realized the warm, soft thing supporting me was Ilyssa. She had my head cradled on her lap. I was surprised and pleased, but I couldn't talk to her or even lift my head.

"I'm so sorry," Chaya said. "I thought the colder weather had killed off the huggers." She shook her head. "Your friend, Chip, is amazing."

I looked a question at her. Why she was telling me about Chip?

"You don't remember? He saved your life."

I blinked.

Ilyssa leaned forward to say, "The coleo stung you so you wouldn't be able to move. You fell. After that, the hugger—"

I rolled my eyes.

She smiled. "Yes, it *is* a strange name for such a hideous thing. Chaya says they're called huggers because they crush their prey. You'd have been mashed if Chip hadn't jumped down from the cage, grabbed the coleo's pincers, and held them open until Chaya dropped a section of her bracelet into the water. The part she used is made from a plant that kills those coleos. Chip is incredibly strong."

I exhaled deeply, and felt my chest go down then up. I also felt something warm against my ribs and Chaya's hand, adjusting the warmth. "These are medicine stones," she said, holding one where I could see it. "We heat them above a tub of gasser spray."

More faces appeared. My other friends came near, looking worried. Chaya warned them not to tire me. As time went by and more feeling returned to my body, she propped me up and gave me tea made from flowers along with a bowl of what she called wild rice. I thought this was disgusting, but she told me apologetically that Stillwaters ate no meat. They did eat certain coleos, though, and if I wanted it, I could have stew made from the hugger who'd tried to kill me.

I never ate a more satisfying meal.

CHAPTER TEN

Mountaineers

The next morning, I felt better, but nearly everyone else felt worse. Jass, Lucan and Adom were worried about the time we'd spent—two nights gone by—without getting any help for our grove. Mellora had the sniffles. Chaya was anxious for her mate, who hadn't returned. Ilyssa…well, that'll take a minute to explain.

I didn't know what to say to her. She'd taken such special care of me, I was confused. Why had she been so kind and concerned?

After breakfast, the others left the big hall, and I got a chance to talk with Ilyssa alone. Her answer wasn't what I expected.

"It's my fault you were hurt," Ilyssa said. "I was so ashamed. I had to make it up to you."

"Your fault? Why?"

"Well, I'm in charge, aren't I? I let you down."

I squinted at her. "*You're* in charge?"

"Of course. I'm the Tropical."

We were moving toward the hall's entrance. I held one reed-covered double door open. "After you, Miss."

Ilyssa noticed my icy tone. "Kor?"

"Thank you for helping me yesterday, Miss Too," I said stiffly, "but you're not in charge of me. My mother sent us on this mission. I'm following her instructions."

"Oh, well, yes, but—"

"I need to thank Chip now," I said, striding away from Ilyssa as quickly as I could.

C hip greeted me at the end of the bridge with a troubled face and a long speech. I tried to tell him thanks in words but ended up slapping his shoulder and pumping his hand, using the gesture I'd learned he used for friendship. He gripped my hand in return, and I thought my bones would break. He really was strong.

More than anything, I wished I could ask him questions about himself. He wasn't a curiosity anymore but a friend who was lost. I had no idea how to get him home, and yet I knew I wouldn't give up trying until I took him there. I owed him that.

Jass and Adom treated me like I was made of thin ice until they were sure I was my old self again. Adom plastered himself to my side, acting like a bodyguard. I told him to knock it off. "I can't let anything else happen to you," he confessed. "Mom would pluck me if I came home without you."

"Hey," I said, tousling his crown feathers, "you're not getting rid of me that easily."

Chaya stood perched atop the jewel box cage inspecting the catch. We flew up to join her. I saw that the fourth coleo had been found.

"What will you do now?" Adom asked her.

"Wait for Brant."

"Will you be safe here alone?"

"I can take care of myself; I'm my father's daughter. Did I tell you he's our chief?"

She hadn't, and we were suitably impressed. "That's why we stayed in the biggest building last night?"

Chaya nodded. "My family lives in the hall when we're here at the marsh."

"So you really wouldn't starve without your coleos?" Adom asked.

"Not starve, no, but without our winnings from the games, Brant and I couldn't build our own nest next year as we planned. I can't thank you enough for helping us, particularly after what you went through, Kor."

I returned her thanks and asked for directions to the Mountaineers. Chaya had already given Jass a map and some wrangler bands in case we ran into more deadly insects.

"As I told Miss Too, he's a sly one," Chaya remarked about Jass. "He'll lead the girls a merry old chase."

"Why were you discussing Jass?" I asked.

"We girls got to talking while you slept. Ilyssa asked for my opinion of him and of you."

"Me? Why me?"

"Ask her."

I already had. Remembering her answer and the point I made about this journey being my responsibility, I went to hurry the others along.

Mountaineers aren't one people, but hunters from every zone who live according to a hero code.

As a nestling, I'd heard their story many times from my mother. It's a source of pride among hunter families. The tale tells of a long-ago queen who wanted every hunter to serve her. She bribed some with riches and others with power, but there were those who wouldn't give her their wings for any price. They retreated to the mountains where they thought they'd be left alone.

The queen declared war on the rebels, who made a last stand against her and her great army at their rocky eyrie above a wide plain.

Outnumbered and surrounded, the Mountaineers begged the sky god to keep them free as he kept the winds. That night, a fierce sandstorm roused myrmecs from their underground city to swarm over the queen's forces on the unprotected plain. The hunters were saved. Calling themselves 'cousins' because all were equal, they vowed to serve the sky god and the cause of freedom ever after.

Since then, the Mountaineer movement spread. There were now many settlements. Following Chaya's map to the nearest one, Jass led us along the river through increasingly broader valleys until the river turned south. There we rested and ate, for beyond this point, we would leave the river and fly north into the drylands.

I enjoyed the flight even though I carried our supplies to prove my strength was back. The wind was with us, brisk enough to arch our wings and increase the distance we could soar without effort. The sun burned warm overhead but the crisp bite of air against my cheeks invigorated me. It was a perfect day for flying, and I thought of how I would have missed this, just days ago. I would never again be flightless, and that thought filled me with joy.

An hour or so into the drylands, we came to piles of rocks sitting in the middle of the plain as though giants had built them by dribbling wet sand between their fingers. Minutes later, we spied two flat-topped pillars capped with walled settlements. I was surprised by how moved I was to know we were approaching a Mountaineer stronghold. Here, I would find the best of my kind, the magnificent, noble Mountaineers. I pictured coming upon them as they gathered together in a courtyard, solemnly chanting to the sky god.

What I saw instead astonished me: Both citadels were topped by bright flags. On the pinnacle closest to us, a line of people stretched from the ground up a long, stone stairway to the entrance gate. Vendor booths near the base of the rock were crowded with customers. Within the walls, row after row of benches set out on a courtyard were already filled with people. More people stood on rooftops of buildings.

At the other citadel, tents of every color rose before more stone structures. Near the edge of the plateau was a crimson pavilion, which held large, richly dressed men and women. They were hunters plumed in brown, black, or gray, but they might have been Tropicals for the brilliant finery they wore. The pavilion overlooked a wooden platform jutting out above the plain.

I signaled my friends to land on the shaded ledge of a high, narrow pillar away from all this activity. Scattered groups of people had found similar perches on other slender rocks.

"What's going on?" Adom asked.

"Must be a festival," I said.

"No, it's a competition," Lucan concluded. "Look there."

I followed his pointing finger toward the second citadel. On the platform, four lines of four men had filed in to stand before a lone man every bit as huge as the Tundran I'd downed. This giant extended his wings and all the others copied him, adjusting their positions where necessary to keep their wingtips from touching. The leader swept back his wings, and so did the others. He raised his fist. Men in the rows went into a sort of a dance, only it wasn't a dance. Though they all made the same moves, their actions were aggressive and fierce, as though they fought invisible enemies.

Suddenly, they lifted off, each rising on one wing beat just as Ilyssa had done by the Grays' temple. It was a stunning sight. At that level, they went on with their movements, then rose again, banked, and streaked away from the citadel, their wings keeping perfect time. Spiraling upward in a line, they soared a high circle, then stooped and rolled, one after the other, reversing direction to return to the platform. When all had landed, they lowered their wings and snapped their heels together.

Cheers rang out from the pavilion. The crowd on the benches in the nearer citadel took up the cry. People on the stairway got noisy and restless because they'd missed the display, so many abandoned the line, taking wing to whatever open spot they could find on distant rocks, just as we had.

Behind me, Jass whooped. "I have got to learn how to do that!"

"Dance?" I asked, turning my head.

"Dance-fight," Jass corrected, eyes gleaming. "That is too cool."

"But why are they doing it?" Ilyssa wanted to know.

"For rank?" Mellora guessed. "I have heard of such contests among Tundran hunters, except those are trials to the death. I don't how rank can be settled in this way, when many men do the same thing and no one is killed."

Adom pointed toward the pavilion where the large hunter who'd started the contest was now talking with two men and a woman. They handed him strips of white, red and black cloth. The man turned away from them and strode to the platform. He signaled to three of the flyers. They stepped forward and he gave them each a cloth, which the men wrapped around their heads. Everyone raised their fists. Then the leader clapped his hands and the men's group left the platform. A minute later, young women with colored ribbons dangling from their flight feathers took their place.

"Oh, now this is getting really interesting," Jass said eagerly, stretching out on the ledge.

"We're wasting time," Ilyssa insisted. "Obviously, the people in charge are at that pavilion. We should go tell them about Sea Grove."

She had a point, but it got lost when we saw that the women were doing something different from the men. We watched the first and third rows turn to face the second and fourth. In pairs, they lifted off, then each flew freely, trying to slice through the other's ribbons by using firestone talons they wore on their feet.

I'd never seen such precision flying. They'd get very close, take a swipe, then lift or dip to avoid damage to their own colors. When a flyer's ribbons were all cut, she flew away. The victor took on a remaining flyer or a pair. The action went so fast, I barely had time to switch my attention from one contest to another before only two females locked in an intense struggle were left.

A horn sounded. Instead of ending the event, the sound produced even greater effort from the final pair. One was a falco like me with dark, pointed wings while the other was larger and had the long crown feathers and light plumage of a golden aquilan.

Now they were using studded bracelets on their wrists to slash at each other. Each had one ribbon left. The falco was tiring, moving too slowly to defend against the aquilan's longer limbs. She couldn't get near enough to make the final cut.

Then, bringing a leg up in an arc, the falco feinted at the aquilan, who backwinged defensively into the falco's reach. With a slice of her wrist bracelet, the falco clipped the last ribbon from the aquilan's leading edge feathers.

The contest was over. The aquilan flew away as the falco landed in triumph on the platform.

Everyone in the pavilion stood up. Everyone *everywhere* stood up. We all yelled our praise. The winner stepped forward to receive a black brow band.

"I think I'm in love," Jass announced.

"Me, too," I agreed. "We could use her help against the Tundrans."

"Maybe she's good at these games," Ilyssa sniffed, "but that doesn't mean she'd be brave against real enemies, and we need more than one person."

Again, Ilyssa had a point. Of course, I didn't want to admit that. "Looks like there's a break in the action. People are leaving the pavilion and the viewing area at the other citadel. Now's our chance to talk to the cousins and get their help."

"I'm staying here," Mellora declared. Ilyssa turned to her with a surprised look. "I'm sorry, Mistress, but I'll go no nearer Tundran hunters. The man who directed the competition was a Tundran. I just *can't*." Mellora lowered her head. "Please don't make me. *Please*, Mistress."

"Of course, I won't make you go if you feel that way. I'm just worried about leaving you alone here."

Chip moved next to Mellora. He tapped his chest.

"You'll stay with her?" Ilyssa asked. "That might be best. It would be hard to explain your appearance."

Chip nodded, and I realized for the first time that he understood us even if we didn't understand him. He screwed up his face, squeezed his throat between thumb and fingers, and squeaked out, "Yesss."

We all stared at him. He grinned.

"I knew it!" Lucan crowed. "He *does* speak out language. He just can't make the sounds like we do very well."

After that, Lucan wouldn't be parted from Chip because he was too interested in learning about him to do anything else. "You don't need me, anyway," Lucan remarked. "I'm not a hunter."

"Well, neither am I," Ilyssa said.

"Maybe you should stay with the others," I suggested.

"No way. I should be there to…well, to…."

"Take charge, Miss Too?"

"Just to be there," Ilyssa answered vaguely. "I want to."

"Enough talk," Jass said. "Let's get moving." He jumped from the ledge and hovered, motioning to Adom. "Last one to the gate is a *loser*."

Ilyssa and I leapt off the rocks at the same time.

CHAPTER ELEVEN

Trials

The gatekeeper at the citadel wouldn't let us pass. Though we told him we were on a mission from our grove, he crossed his arms and said, "No visitors allowed at Heroes' Eyrie. Spectators stay on Ladies' Butte."

"But what about those tents?" Adom argued. "The people using them don't live here."

"The tents are for competitors in the tournament," the gatekeeper said.

"So," Ilyssa pressed, "if we compete in an event, we can get in to talk to the head Mountaineers?"

The gatekeeper, a stocky buteo, snorted. "Girl, you're no hunter, and you're a Tropical, at that. *You* couldn't enter any event. As for talking to the Senior Cousins...." He broke into noisy laughter at the thought.

I stepped in front of Ilyssa, whose face had gone red. I was afraid she'd make things worse if she spoke again. Pointing to Jass and myself, I said, "We're hunters, and we'd like to enter the tournament, but we haven't chosen the event. Is there somewhere we could see a schedule?"

The gatekeeper rolled his eyes. "There's a list posted on the side of this gate—*if* you can read." He chuckled at his own wit and stepped back into the shade, leaving us to fume in the heat of the noonday sun.

"I have never been treated this way!" Ilyssa hissed, outraged. "Who do these people think they are?"

"Mountaineers," I murmured as I went round to inspect the sign, which was written in the Woodlander runes I knew. "Scat! This looks complicated."

The list of events for the three-day Remembrance Tourney went on and on, each contest divided by age and gender. There were "Airs," which I took to be those dance-fights the men did, and "Ailereons," which meant nothing to me until I saw that the timing of the women's event we'd watched matched that category. Weapons competitions on the ground and in the air—archery, darting, talonry, spear throwing and sling targeting—were clear enough, but we didn't have the gear or the training for those.

Jass thought he might try his wings at obstacle flying and suggested I enter a speed competition ("You did great with that Tundran, Kor."), but I suspected I couldn't outfly big Mountaineers in top condition. It seemed Jass was our only hope until Adom slipped under my wing to check the list. He muttered, "...Pangolin Hunt Trials. Pangolins! *I* can handle pangs. I've had lots of practice."

"When did you get anywhere near a pangolin?" I scoffed.

"Every time I went to visit Kes. Her father's Sea Grove's pang master. He taught me about them."

"Kes?"

"You met Kes on the roost by our nest the day you found Chip."

I pictured the girl who'd asked about elves. "She's the daughter of the pangolin keeper?"

"Yes. I just said that. This will be easy," Adom said, snapping his fingers. He drew me aside, whispering slyly, "I can use one of the bands Chaya gave us. There's a patch with myrmec scent."

I thought about pangolins and myrmecs. To detect myrmec swarms, our grove kept pangolins prowling the walls at all times. The large, armored animals were twice the size of an average myrmec, so they could easily kill and eat one scout. Faced with an army of myrmecs, pangolins rolled themselves into balls and waited until the danger passed.

Our Elders said stopping myrmec scouts from returning to their underground cities would keep a swarm from coming to our grove. Most of the time that seemed to work, except when something really big—ground shake or windstorm or wildfire—got the myrmecs excited.

They were like a black sea that had no shore I'd heard, though I'd never seen a full myrmec swarm. They ate everything in their path that wasn't plated, spined, quilled or poisonous until they decided to stop. Small swarms were common. Thousands of myrmecs suddenly went on the march to a new place, maybe because they'd outgrown their old city. Who knows?

My father expected more swarming now that the weather was turning colder every year. Just as the Tundrans had been pushed from the icy lands, the myrmecs were looking for warmer territory, too. Pangolins were more important than ever.

The problem was that pangs were strong and willful, hard to control when they scented prey. It didn't take any prodding to get them to fight, using teeth and claws that could slice a man's body in two. When they were angry, pangs held their plates open, turning their whole bodies into living blades.

So why was I even thinking of letting Adom enter a pangolin competition?

"I have to do it," Adom answered my thoughts. "When I win, I'll get to meet the cousins at the pavilion, won't I? Then I can tell them about the raiders attacking our grove."

"It's too dangerous," Ilyssa said.

"So, Adom, this Kes is your girlfriend?" Jass asked.

"Yeah," Adom answered immediately.

My little brother had a girlfriend. When had that happened? I needed to spend more time with Adom, I decided.

Adom rapped on the gate. "You there! I want to enter the pangolin hunt trials." After a moment, the gatekeeper reappeared and shrugged. "You're young, but there's no minimum age. Where's your contribution?"

"Contribution?"

The gatekeeper looked like he was fighting the urge to roll his eyes again. "Every contestant has to offer something of value to the Eyrie," he recited in a bored voice. "An entrance fee. That's the rule."

Ilyssa stepped forward. The gatekeeper's left eyebrow went up, followed in an instant by the right one when he saw the teardrop pearl in her palm.

"This should do," she said with chin held high, "for admission to the pangolin hunt trials *and* the obstacle flying."

"There's just the one other thing," the gatekeeper said slowly and with obvious pleasure after pocketing the pearl. "No contestant supporters are allowed. It's participants *only*."

"All those people working around the tents aren't dressed for competition," Adom challenged.

"Neither are you," the gatekeeper shot back.

"They're servants," Ilyssa guessed, squinting hard at him, "aren't they?"

"Pages and squires," the gatekeeper admitted.

"It just so happens that I'm a squire," Ilyssa said, pointing to Adom. "His. And Kor is Jass'."

The guard pursed his lips, but he handed us a map and numbered cloths with neck strings before he waved us through to the tenting ground. "Stay by the walls or on the path to the platform while you're at Heroes' Eyrie. No poking around the buildings or the pavilion. The guards there aren't as sweet-natured as I am."

We left him chortling merrily to himself.

Adom's event was scheduled after Jass', which would take place at the other citadel. Jass smirked when he saw the location. "Ladies' Butte? What's a *butte*? I know what a lady's butt is."

"Ha," I said, "ha."

"You have no sense of humor," Jass returned. "I, on the other hand, am ripe with wit."

"Overripe," Ilyssa observed, wrinkling her nose. "Study this map," she told Jass, who leaned against the Eyrie's inner wall. "This is the course you're to fly. See here? It begins at the biggest building, goes through the courtyard and under the arch before it makes a hard right turn to follow the lane between smaller buildings. When the lane ends, you fly over the inner wall and get past barricades as fast as you can. The race ends at the main gate. Whoever has the best time comes to the platform here on Heroes' Eyrie. Got that?"

Jass was eying a pretty girl wearing the black tunic and trousers of a competitor. She smiled slowly over her shoulder at him. "Yeah, sure."

"Pay attention!" Ilyssa warned. "If you mess this up, we might never get in to see those Senior Cousins."

"Hey, squire," Adom said to Ilyssa, but he said that with a smile, "what about me? Don't I need coaching?"

"You'll do fine," Ilyssa told him. "You'll do *wonderfully*, Adom.

Besides," she confessed, "I don't know anything about pangolins."

"I do," said a male voice from behind me.

I jumped. Not only was the voice right beside my ear, it was *that* sort of voice, a voice used to command.

The voice belonged to young aquilan in the standard, black uniform. He had a red brow band wrapped around his white crown. Beside him stood *the* girl—the falco who'd bested the female aquilan. I recognized her plumage. She was incredibly beautiful close up.

"You," I said to her, surprised.

"Do I have dirt on my face?" her honey-voice inquired.

I shook my head, confused. "No."

"Then you must be staring at my badge." She gestured toward her black brow band. "I'm Serena."

"K—Kor," I stammered.

Jass pushed off the wall. "Jass Gos," he said.

Serena nodded toward the number he'd hung around his neck. "You're a contestant?"

"Obstacle flying."

"I'm Adom, and I'm in the pangolin hunt trials," my brother said to the still-unnamed male. "What do you know about them?"

"Everything. I'm their trainer."

Adom shook his head. "Can't be. It takes years to become a pangolin master."

Serena smiled. "This is Boran. He's the First Cousin's nephew, and it doesn't take him years to do anything."

Boran shrugged. He said, "We noticed your group. You're not wearing the colors of any Mountaineer settlement we recognize."

"We're not Mountaineers," Adom said. "We came here to get help."

"For what?"

"To save our grove—Sea Grove—from Tundrans."

"Why should we do that?" Boran wondered.

Adom's head jerked back. "Because you're Mountaineers! That's what you do, isn't it?"

"It was, but times change. We make fewer rescues every year. Can't take on the world, you know. Now, we mostly look after our own people."

I frowned. "But aren't we all your people, all of us hunters?"

Boran lifted his snowy head. "Hardly. Only the best hunters get to be Mountaineers. We have more applicants than we can admit. There's a waiting list."

Ilyssa said, "I'm Miss Ilyssa Too. We'd really appreciate the chance to talk to the people in charge here."

"Look," Boran said to Adom, "I'll take you on a tour of the pangolin pens, offer up some pointers on their habits. Maybe that will give you an edge."

"Excuse me," Ilyssa said with irritation rasping her voice, "but can we stick to the subject? How do we get in to see the Senior Cousins?"

Boran turned to Serena. "Will you handle this?"

"If you like."

"Meet me at the pang pens in a few minutes," Boran told Adom. "I need to speak with someone first. Nice chatting with you," he tossed out to the rest of us just before hailing a passing male aquilan.

Serena looked up at the sky. "It's later than I thought. I have to leave for another match. Bye, boys." She sprinted down the path.

"That…those…*people* were the rudest I've ever met!" Ilyssa seethed. She whirled on me. "Those are the ones who are going to save our grove? Those conceited, selfish, useless—"

"They didn't seem so bad," Adom cut in. "It'll be a big help to learn about the pangs here."

"Not bad? They were horrible," Ilyssa sputtered. "That Boran jerk wouldn't even talk to me. He treated me like...like..."

"A servant?" I suggested. "Or the way a Tropical treats a Woodlander?"

Ilyssa's mouth opened. Then it closed. Her eyes blazed. "Kor Tiercel, I'll never forgive you for that." She turned on her heel and lifted off, flying in the direction of the ledge where we'd left the others.

"You've got a winning way with girls, Kor," Jass told me, clucking his tongue.

"He's backward," Adom confided.

I slapped my palm to my forehead.

"So I shouldn't go see Boran?" Adom asked seriously.

"Go," Jass said. "Could pay off. I'll fly over to Ladies' Butt with you. It's almost time for my event."

J ass put in a good race, but he couldn't equal the speed of flyers familiar with the territory who knew all the tricks. After the winner flew to the platform on Heroes' Eyrie, Jass went with me to the pangolin pens, which had been moved from the citadel's walls to the base of Ladies' Butte because of the tournament.

Adom was in good spirits. Boran had kept his word and given him a tour, describing the animals and their habits. According to Boran, a gentle female named Salli was the one Adom should pick. Adom took his advice.

We studied Salli through the slats of her pen. She was curled into a ball, sleeping. She looked peaceful enough, but it was hard to see much of her in that position.

"You're sure about this?" I asked Adom again.

"No problem. All I have to do is lead her out to the trial grounds and—"

"Wait a minute. The trials aren't inside the walls? *Where* are the hunt grounds?"

"Out there." Adom waved his arm toward the open plain.

"No," I said flatly, repeating the words I'd heard from my parents hundreds of times. "We *never* go to open land on foot."

Jass rocked his head from side to side and then made a face. "When did you turn into your mother?"

"It's not that far," Adom argued. "See? Right there by those markers is where the trials start."

"Oh…" A field of thin, sandstone slabs began around a hundred paces away. There were a lot of markers, but a person out there could see in every direction, certainly far enough to get away before any insects might surprise him. We'd faced greater danger at the swamp. "Oh, that's not so bad."

Adom grinned. "You worry too much. It's easy. I lead Salli to the starting line, take her around the markers, and get her to find some myrmec scent that's been put there." He lowered his voice to a whisper. "I can cheat if I have to using the scent band." Talking normally, he added, "When she smells myrmec, she stiffens out, nose to tail pointing at it. The people who are counting the time stop, and because Salli and I are the fastest, we win." Adom smiled approvingly at his sleeping pangolin partner.

As though she knew we were talking about her, Salli woke and stretched, unfurling into the longest pang I'd ever seen. Staring wide-eyed over her endless back, I watched a man stride out onto the plain. He lifted a horn to his lips and called participants to the pangolin trials.

CHAPTER TWELVE

The Myrmec City

Men—not fledglings like Adom—began turning up to take charge of their pangolins. Equipped with rhino-hide leads, they left the pen area, staying well apart because their animals snarled at each other when they got too close together. Angry pangolins raised their plates, causing more than one handler to leap aside abruptly to avoid losing half a wing or leg.

I rubbed my forehead. Adom insisted on going through with this. When a keeper took the lock off Salli's cage, Adom stepped inside eagerly, speaking to her in a friendly, reassuring way.

She studied him from the corner of her slanted eye. Adom went to slip the lead's collar over her head, but she drew back. Pangs don't have much by way of facial expressions, but I swear that one was amused. Salli lifted her head and made a gurgling noise that had to be pangolin snickering.

"Adom, give it up," I urged. "We'll find another way to get the Senior Cousins' attention."

"No! I can do this!" Adom stamped his foot, and then reached the collar toward Salli. She thrust her nose into the corner. Adom tried again.

"No doubt about it: He's your brother," Jass observed. "Stubborn as they come."

I sighed, then sucked in my breath. Salli's plates were rising.

Adom reached carefully between plates to scratch her neck. Salli arched her back before facing Adom, lowering her plates graciously so he could put the collar on her.

It was too soon to rejoice. The instant Adom snugged up the loop, Salli took off, jerking him around and pulling him out of the pen. Picking a fight with the nearest caged pangolin, Salli hissed, raised her plates and shook them. Scat! She was scaring *me*. I had no idea what the other pangolin would do.

The challenged pang rolled into a ball. Salli sniffed and yanked Adom along the aisle and out of the enclosure. Jass and I followed, wondering what would come next.

Ilyssa was what came next. She and Lucan stood at the front of the roped-off spectators' platform, waving and whistling. Adom flashed a grin before he had to concentrate on gripping Salli's lead with both hands to keep up with the loping pangolin.

Adom didn't have to give way to other contestants; their pangolins fled from Salli's path. She switched to a prancing gait, lifting her feet with each step, showing off while she held the other animals at bay. Her final act of contempt was to inspect the ground at the center of the starting line with great care before turning in a circle and lying down, curling her tail around her. Adom scrambled into position at her side.

Jass and I went to join Ilyssa and Lucan, but a guard stopped us from lifting the rope. "Unless you have a ticket," he said, "this is a restricted area—paid seating only."

"But our friends are there," Jass said, pointing toward Ilyssa and Lucan.

"Do they have tickets for you?"

"No...I don't know," Jass answered.

"I'll check." The guard did that, bending over Lucan, who looked toward Ilyssa. With a sweet smile, she shook her head and returned her attention to the starting line.

Scuffing at the dust, Jass and I were on our own. I couldn't quite bring myself to sit out there in the open, so I shifted from foot to foot, noticing Jass did the same. For all his brave talk, he didn't like being on the ground any better than I did.

We hadn't long to wait, though. A man came to the line, maybe the same Tundran who directed the flyers earlier. He raised then lowered one arm, and the first man/pangolin pair was off. Chanters counted their time.

The team rounded several markers, which were bigger than they'd looked from the pens. Disappearing from my sight line where the ground dipped down, the pair was gone. How frustrating it was to be so low I couldn't see the entire course! I'd halfway convinced myself to fly back to the ledge or to find a perch on the walls when the chanters reached forty-two and stopped. The first team returned to receive applause from spectators.

It was hot and bright under the afternoon sun. I got bored after three other pairs had gone through the trials. In the middle of the line, Adom still had two teams ahead of him.

My mind drifted away. *How long will Ilyssa stay mad at me? What's going on at Sea Grove? Will we ever get help from the Mountaineers? When can I find something to eat?*

Jass elbowed me. It was Adom and Salli's turn.

The second the Tundran's arm dropped, Salli was off like a hurled spear, dragging Adom along in her wake. She didn't bother going around the markers but charged the first one. Lowering her nose for an instant as the column collapsed into dust, she plunged onward, and I suddenly realized the markers were nothing more than heaps of sand and dirt. Their smooth, flat surfaces looked man-made, but they were natural. These were myrmec tubes, the air and heat vents for underground tunnels. Adom wouldn't need to supply any false myrmec scent. He was running over the top of their city.

I lifted off, and so, it seemed, did everyone else. The air was filling with flyers not looking in Adom's direction. They were winging away from the plain at top speed. In the middle of this chaos, I couldn't spot Adom.

But I could hear the sound of thousands of branches breaking under ice. No, that wasn't it, I told myself as I dodged flyers and made for the markers. I was hearing clicking from myrmecs outraged by the damage to their city.

When I found him, Adom was barely visible at the bottom of a pile of myrmecs, pinned under their weight, arms wrapped around a rock to keep himself from being pulled into a hole. Those myrmecs weren't trying to eat him on the spot, at least. For some reason, most of them were waving their antennae at the air, as though expecting something to arrive from above. With every extra second it took me to get to Adom, more myrmecs emerged from their tunnels.

I called to my brother, but I couldn't hear if he answered; the clicking was maddeningly loud. Poised just above the myrmecs, I reach down to lift one off the pile, but it turned on me, jaws shearing at my arm. I let go and pulled up.

Jass was beside me then, and so were Ilyssa and Lucan. "Why aren't they biting Adom?" Lucan shouted.

"Just get them off him!" I yelled, hauling on the middle section of the nearest myrmec. This was no more successful than my first try. Every time I got hold of one, it'd fight me, and I had to release it because

I had no weapon.

Lucan did. He stabbed a myrmec with his firestone knife. The others went wild and launched themselves at him. I tried again to reach Adom, who was nearly buried by black bodies.

Suddenly, the air around me filled with men and women, flashes of color blurring with motion. They used arrows and spears on the myrmecs. Gore splattered me; I shoved it off my face. After blinking my eyes clear, I saw Adom being lifted out of the myrmec mound by a white-headed aquilan in a gold-edged, blue robe.

There was a whistle, and the Mountaineers rose up from the plain, turning to fly toward Heroes' Eyrie. I called to Jass, Lucan and Ilyssa, pointing toward the departing flyers. "They've got Adom. Let's go!" My friends heard and followed me.

We left the myrmecs below, the live ones clicking furiously; the dying, twitching in their death throes. The last thing I saw was Salli, gorging on myrmecs.

When I reached the landing platform, I pushed through the crowd to my brother. I hugged him, feeling so glad he was alive I couldn't speak. My eyes welled up when I pulled back to inspect him. Other than some scratches on his face, he looked all right.

"Now you know how I felt yesterday when that coleo nearly squashed you," Adom choked out.

The aquilan who'd rescued Adom bent down to address him. All the chatter on the platform stopped when the man asked, "Lad, what were you trying to do with that animal?"

"Hunting trial," Adom said indignantly.

"A pregnant pangolin's craving for myrmecs is uncontrollable."

Adom pointed to Boran. "He told me to take her."

The aquilan glowered at Boran, who produced a sickly smile. "The boy said he wanted a challenge."

The big man held out one hand. "Your colors," he said to Boran.

"Uncle?"

"Remove your brow band. You're barred from the tourney and your honors are forfeit. Oh, and you're relieved of pangolin duties henceforth."

"But—"

"Silence, Boran," the aquilan rumbled. "Your behavior toward these strangers shames us. Leave the pavilion." He turned to Adom. "Who are you? Where are you from?"

Adom introduced the two of us, and then motioned Ilyssa, Jass and Lucan to come forward. The crowd parted for them until we were grouped together. "We're from Sea Grove," Adom explained. "We came here to see the Senior Cousins."

"I am Loran, First Cousin," the aquilan told us.

"Then you're the one we want to talk to," Adom said. "Our grove is under attack from Tundrans. We need your help to fight them."

Loran rubbed his chin. "We're in the midst of a tournament."

Adom got angry. "I know! Your gatekeeper made us pay to play your stupid games just so we could ask for your help. While you're sitting here, watching people *pretending* to be warriors, my people are fighting for their lives.

"My mother told us to come here. She trusted you. She's always taught Kor and me to respect you. I wanted to grow up to be just like you, but now I don't know: Are you still Mountaineers or is this a Tropical city?"

Loran smiled. "Your friend takes exception to that statement."

I looked at Ilyssa. Her crest was up.

"Today, I saw a Tropical behave with more valor than my nephew." Loran dipped his great, white head to Ilyssa before excusing himself to speak with two other aquilans. When he returned, he crooked a finger at a stately, aged woman. "Mered, my horn." She looked a question at him. "The horn," he repeated brusquely.

The platform cleared except for our group and Loran. When the woman carried in the massive, curling horn of some animal, Loran said just to us, "On this Remembrance Day, you've laid grave charges against us, reminding me of a most important fact: Mountaineers live to preserve freedom." Raising his voice and turning in place with arms extended, he cried, "We are Mountaineers!"

All the people in the pavilion roared their agreement. Loran took hold of the horn and strode to the edge of the platform, calling out in a voice so strong I'm sure it carried all the way to Mellora and Chip, "This day, we honor the young wing, Adom Tiercel, who knows what it means to be Mountaineer. He risked his life for the freedom of his people. To save them, we go to war!" Loran blew the horn, and everyone I could see on both citadels and the surrounding rocks cheered and waved their hands. Young men and women took flight until the sky glittered with their excited soaring.

And so my brother became a hero, just as I always knew he would.

It took no more than an hour for the first wave of hunters to leave Heroes' Eyrie, heading at full speed for Sea Grove. Adom went with them, of course, and so did Jass. Before they left, I had a talk with Jass.

"Take care of Adom," I told my best friend.

"He has an army of Mountaineers for protection, and he can handle himself," Jass reminded me. "Opening the myrmec patch on his band was really smart."

"I'm just glad the scent didn't make them angrier."

"Adom's girlfriend's father told him myrmecs hate their neighbors but tolerate lone strangers until they consult their queen. Guess that's true."

Jass was barely managing to keep a foot on the ground, obsessed as he was with his new gear. The Mountaineer girl, Serena, had brought him firestone talons and a spear, saying she needed a wingman now that she despised Boran. Jass kept raising his wings over his head while he gazed down, surveying his magnificence and gaining a little air each time. "War! You're sure you won't come?"

"Can't." I shook my head. "There's still Chip to take home."

"About that," Jass said, finally grounded as he adjusted his breech ties to hide the coleo-clipped shin feathers on his left leg, "where will you go?"

"Lucan has some ideas."

Those of us who were staying made camp in the tenters' area, thanks to Loran, who gave us two tents, one for the girls and one for the boys. Both tents were tall, red, and richly furnished with benches, tables, thick rugs, and bedding fleeces of some wooly, white animal that I'd been told lived near the ice lands. So far, servers from the Eyrie's hall had brought food for us twice. I was glad to get meat at last.

Mellora argued against moving to a place where there were Tundrans, but she had to give in when we told her Loran considered us his personal guests. With the preparations for war and the sudden end of the tournament, Chip's entrance into the Eyrie went unnoticed. He wrapped himself in Ilyssa's cloak and disguised his wings as baggage. Chip stayed cloaked and near the tents, talking to Lucan, who claimed to understand a lot of Chip's speech now. Lucan promised to tell us what he knew about Chip over supper tonight.

We'd dine in Miss Too's tent; Ilyssa had forgiven me. Mountaineers weren't so bad now, in her opinion, and neither were the rest of us hunters—for the moment.

CHAPTER THIRTEEN

Rainbow Stone

F resh from the baths at Ladies' Butte, Ilyssa greeted us for supper looking the part of the elegant, Tropical hostess. She'd arranged to get her traveling clothes washed, she said, so she had on the gown she'd been wearing when we sneaked away from her family's party. She also had the teardrop pearl, which Loran returned to her. It seemed the greedy gatekeeper hadn't been told to take offerings from people competing in the tournament. He'd come up with that scheme on his own. Ilyssa smirked when she reported seeing the gatekeeper and Boran cleaning the latrines.

She looked *great*. When I told her so, she gave me a surprised smile that made me feel good inside. I'd been missing Jass and Adom, wishing they were still with us, but I stopped feeling sad after that. I ate until I was stuffed, comforted by the good company around me.

Mellora's sniffles had turned into a cold. After we ate, Ilyssa told her to go to her sleeping place. The rest of us moved toward the front of the tent and lay there on the thick rugs, keeping our voices low while planning our next move.

Lucan explained what he'd learned about Chip. "He understands us best when we talk as slow and deep as we can." Demonstrating this, Lucan did a fair imitation of Loran's voice but drew out the sounds and left long gaps between words. Chip nodded his encouragement.

"Chip can't speak like us without hurting his throat," Lucan continued. "When he talks in his normal voice, I understand a lot of the words. Most of the time, we use a kind of sign language. His sign for me is a hand opening and closing like a mouth." Lucan tapped his fingers against his thumb. Chip rumbled with laughter.

"What am I?" Ilyssa asked.

"You're a hug, like this." Lucan clasped his forearms together. Ilyssa beamed.

"Me," I said. "What does Chip call me?"

Lucan put his wrists together and flapped his fingers. "You're wings."

I liked that. "Mellora?"

"Her symbol is palm to the cheek. Chip thinks she's pretty."

Ilyssa said after something of a pause, "What's his real name? We've been calling him 'Chip' all this time. He must have a proper name."

Lucan ran a hand through his crown feathers. "He does, but it's long, and I can't say it right. To me, it sounds like a hiss. He doesn't mind being called Chip, though."

"So where is he from?" I asked. "And why did he come to our grove?"

"He got lost after…." Lucan grimaced before revealing the rest. "He came from the sky."

"He lives in the *sky*? You can't have that right," I objected.

"Yes, I do. Every time I ask him, he points up. He came from there to here looking for a stone."

"What kind of stone?" Ilyssa wanted to know. "And…and is he a sky *god*?"

Lucan sighed. "Far as I can tell, he's not a god. I mean, he can't do amazing things, can he?"

"He's very strong," Ilyssa reminded us all. Trying her best to talk as Lucan had, Ilyssa asked Chip about being a god.

He shook his head. Sweeping his hand around in a circle, he ended by thumping his own chest. Chip was just like us, the gesture said to me.

Lucan, Ilyssa and I relaxed. It's scary to think you're talking to a god, but I couldn't imagine how a person might live in the sky, especially one whose wings weren't part of his body. I tried to picture Chip floating on clouds or tiptoeing on the tiny lights up there at night, and I chuckled at my silly thoughts.

"All I can tell you is what he's told me. I don't understand it, either," Lucan said. "There's some problem where he comes from. Chip needs to find a stone to help his people escape it."

"What kind of stone is so special?" I asked.

Lucan plucked at his own tunic front, then pointed to his neck. He said, "Chip? Show them." Chip responded by pulling on the fastener of his garment, loosening it to expose a necklace. He brought this forward, holding it out so we could see it. A linked chain held a pendant of bright metal with many square-edged parts and lines all around. At first, I thought it had been carved into the shape of a flying person, but a closer look convinced me the stone had formed that way.

"It's so beautiful—all those colors." Ilyssa peered at the stone. "Blue, green, purple, gold, pink."

"Just like a Tropical party," I put in.

Ilyssa smiled, but kept on. "If Chip already has a stone, why does he need another?"

"That's not the right stone. He brought that one with him. He needs one like it from here," Lucan replied.

"He's a shaman." Mellora came over to join us. We all looked up at her. "I couldn't sleep, and I was curious," she told Ilyssa. "That," she added, pointing to Chip's necklace, "is a rainbow stone. Shamans among my people use them to talk with the gods."

"How do we get a rainbow stone?" Lucan asked. "Chip has no idea where to look."

Mellora knelt before Chip, gazing at his treasure. "They come from hollows in dying mountains."

I'd never heard of dying mountains and neither had anyone else, I guessed, by the blank expressions on their faces.

"You don't know of these? Dying mountains burn with fever, so they throw off their snow blankets, uncovering dry, cracked skin. They groan and belch smoke. Sometimes, you can see where they're coughing up smelly, sick breaths through mud."

I *had* heard of such a place. My father discovered it on a hunt, and he told the family about it. The stink from bubbling mud pits dazed him for a time; he said he became too dizzy to fly. He had to crawl away, despite the risk of attackers on land. Yes, there was a dying mountain close enough for my father to visit.

While I told that story, Ilyssa looked distracted, barely listening to my words. This annoyed me until she said, "Faster-than-light travel." After that, I was irritated because I didn't know what she was talking about.

Ilyssa squeezed her eyelids shut and rapped on her forehead, only to moan, "I *wish* I could remember. It's there inside my head, but I can't get it out."

Concerned, Mellora reached a hand to Ilyssa's forehead. Ilyssa waved her off. "No, I'm not ill. I'm trying to remember things from the Cave of the Gods."

She had all our attention now. Though it was forbidden to talk about the Cave, Ilyssa seemed determined to do that.

"Don't!" Lucan pleaded. "Don't speak of it. Don't make the gods angry." His eyes had gone white-edged with fear.

Ilyssa held both hands to her head. She seemed to be struggling with herself. Finally, she sighed and stayed silent.

Our evening ended shortly after that; we all needed sleep. At first light, I'd ask Loran where we could find a dying mountain, but I lay awake for a long time, trying to picture a grove floating in the sky and other people like Chip living there. In the clouds, what would they do with a stone? Where did they need to go, and why did they have to race the sun? When I finally slept, my dreams were troubled.

In the morning, I went to the Eyrie's gathering hall, a simple, flat-roofed, stone structure. Inside the entrance, there was a blue-green metal circle hanging from cords—a marvelous thing. Large, metal objects are rare because they cost so much. Only oresmiths knew how to make metal into useful shapes, and we had no oresmiths in Sea Grove.

When I tapped on the circle, it made a sound. Next thing I knew, the woman who'd brought Loran his horn was beside me. She didn't look angry about the noise, so I asked for Loran, learning he had gone to Sea Grove. During his absence, she was First Cousin. She said I should call her Mered.

I told her we were seeking a stone for our grove's shaman so he could thank the gods for the Mountaineers' help when we returned home. This was stretching the truth if not an outright lie, but I didn't want to explain about Chip.

Mered seemed pleased by the idea and knew of a dying mountain, though she found that description amusing. Her lips turned up before she told me gray mountains lay northwest, only half a day's flight. We must follow a canyon through hills until we came to a wide, green valley. We would see the gray mountains from there. To reach the canyon, we had to pass over the myrmec city.

Thinking about Adom and the myrmecs, I couldn't keep from asking why a pangolin trial had been set in that place.

"That was the test," she replied. "Hunters must be able to move undetected, even on foot. Myrmecs are a part of everyday life here. Perhaps we lose sight of the danger."

I thanked Mered and the Mountaineers for their hospitality. She wished us well and instructed me to stop by the larder, where I could get food for our journey. I did that, and then returned to the tents, finding my friends ready to leave.

Chip had to show his wings when we took off, but no one followed us, so that was all right. Though the time we spent over the myrmec city was nerve wracking, nothing frightening happened. The myrmecs we saw ignored us as we flew over them.

Soon enough, we found the canyon, which held a river during the rainy season but was dry now. At the grove, not a day passed without fog, mist or rain. But here, everything around us was parched.

Inside the canyon, the sun roasted our backs. Lucan's black feathers gleamed in the glare, and Chip's furry head went dark with sweat. Mellora's face had a miserable, desperate look to it.

Ilyssa was happy. "Isn't this great weather?" she called out.

Lucan howled back, "Only if you're a Tropical!"

I noticed that Chip was flying high today. His wings seemed stronger under this fierce sun. I still couldn't understand those wings, but there they were, and so was Chip, who shouldn't be real, either.

Heat baked my head too much to think deep thoughts, so I watched the ground go by. The canyon was filled with lizards—not too big, but heavily armored and spiked to protect themselves from long-tailed scorpions. A cloud of flies like a black cloak forced us out of its path. I couldn't wait to be away from that place.

We finally reached the valley, which was cool and pleasant. Rhinos grazed on thick grass. A quilled cat with long fangs crouched behind thorn trees, stalking the rhinos, probably. She growled at our passing shadows.

The gray mountains were ahead of us, and so were dark blue lakes surrounded by slim trees with autumn-bright leaves. Though we were tired and thirsty, I urged everyone to keep flying. I didn't want to risk an attack on the ground. At last, even I wanted to stop when the trees parted for a silvery, fast-flowing stream. We landed on its north bank.

"You, there," a stern, male voice called. "Outta my fishin' crick!"

Standing on a fallen tree spanning the water, a big, white-and-brown pandion with a spear flared his long wings. He thumped the butt of the spear on the log. "I mean it, now. Git."

"Pardon, sir," Lucan said politely, "but we—"

"What in tarnation is *that*?" the pandion demanded, pointing at Chip.

Angry, Lucan drew himself up to his full height, which still wasn't much compared to a grown pandion. He said, "Chip is our friend, a traveler from far away."

"Oh, well, if he's your *friend*…" The pandion laughed, but not in a nasty way. I was beginning to suspect his gruffness was mostly for show.

"What makes this your creek?" I asked him.

"Been fishin' here all my life. I reckon that makes it mine." Looking down his hooked nose to regard us with narrow-set, yellow eyes, the pandion took our measure. "Just passin' through, are ya?"

"We need water and rest," Mellora said with a tearful edge to her voice.

I turned to look at her. She was pale, and her shoulders slumped with weariness.

"Aw now, don' start cryin', lil missy," the pandion said, gently this time. "Get yer filla both, but not here. Mosey down the bank a ways." He waggled his free hand at us. "Make that a hundred paces or so to the bend where the water spills into the prettiest little swimmin' hole you ever did see—and you won' be scarin' off my trout."

Now that he'd identified the whooshing sound, I could hear the falls. I felt homesick for the grove.

"An' you, boy," the pandion said to me, "keep yer chin up. I 'spect you've a ways to go afore yer day is through."

"Why do you say that?" Ilyssa asked.

The pandion stared at her. "Whooee! We don' git Tropicals in this necka the woods. Don' git visitors 't all. You folk got business round here?"

"We're going to the gray mountains to find a stone," Lucan said. "It's a metal with many colors and hard angles. Do you know where we should look?"

The pandion scratched the back of his neck. "You fixin' for a fight, boy?"

"Fight?" Lucan repeated.

"'Cuz that's what you'll git if yer huntin' for metal. Round these parts, oresmiths take that stuff verra seriously. They don' like strangers stickin' their noses where they don' belong. They're a private bunch, the oresmiths. Think they got big secrets to keep about where they git their metal and how they make it into things."

"Do these oresmiths control all the gray mountains?" I asked.

"Pretty much. They wouldn' take kindly to yer trespassin' on their ground."

"We *must* get the stone," Lucan said. "Is there a way to avoid the oresmiths?

"Hire yerselves a Chiro guide. That's what I'd do. Chiros got their ways of movin' around on the sly like."

"Herry?" a booming, female voice called. "You caught lunch yet?"

"Jest about," the pandion lied, giving the stream a quick check. He said to us, "That's the missus. She's got a powerful appetite. I'd best be about my business now."

"One more question," Ilyssa put in. "How do we find a Chiro?"

Herry lifted his spear. Eyes intent on catching lunch, he told us, "Long afore you find them, they'll find you." He raised his head to wink at us. "They surely will."

CHAPTER FOURTEEN

Chiros

The waterfall pool was cool, clear and irresistible. It wasn't long before we were in it, we boys, at least.

Leaning against Chip's wings in a patch of sunlight, Ilyssa happily soaked up more heat. Mellora sat on the pool's edge, dangling her feet in the water but remaining watchful.

As for Lucan and me, we'd checked the place for insects and other nasty things, then stripped to our breeches and waded in under the fall, which was cozy—not too tall, just half again a man's height with a flow that didn't batter our heads. Chip had been more cautious, inspecting the pool from the rocks above until he shrugged and shucked off his one-piece garment to stand there in short, blue pants. Suddenly, he leapt over the top, grabbing his knees with his hands, landing with a giant splash that brought outraged howls from the splattered girls. What a move! If I'd tried that, my wings would have hit first, filling with water for a painful back wrench.

Without his clothes, Chip's appearance was confusing. I still couldn't decide how old he was. When we met, I thought of him as downy-young. Then, as we traveled, I started to see him as older, particularly after he saved my life. Now, his featherless back and legs made me think of him more as the helpless furred boy from the grove.

He soon changed my mind again. Rising from the water, Chip

palmed a heroic blast of water at Lucan and me, nearly bowling us over. Of course, we fought back. While I sent fast bursts to distract him, Lucan sneaked around to push down on Chip's shoulders and dunk him. Chip went under, then shot up from the water, jumping almost fully into the air before he fell back laughing. His legs, it seemed, were as strong as his arms.

When our water fight was done, Chip had only to slick back his head fur and dress, but Lucan and I stretched out our wings to dry them. I wondered if Ilyssa would volunteer to preen my back coverts—it's hard for a person to get at those himself—but she beckoned to Lucan. He lay on his stomach while she smoothed the vanes flat with a practiced hand. "I do this all the time for my sister," she remarked wistfully. "Sorlyn has such lovely color. Her crest's going more golden every year."

Mellora waved me over to a spot by her side. "I'll be losing my colored feathers soon," she observed to Ilyssa while working on my back, "and turning white."

"All white?" I inquired over my shoulder.

"Mmm. In winter, we phasians molt to look like snow. It's handy for hiding from beasts and Tundran hunters."

"Oh, too bad," Ilyssa said sadly. "Your plumage is so pretty."

The way she said that got me thinking. "You don't like being all white?"

Ilyssa made a face. "It's just plain and dull." She straightened the last of Lucan's secondaries. "Even all-black feathers are prettier. See here? When the light hits them just right, they shine like that rainbow stone."

How could Ilyssa think she was "plain and dull"? I didn't have time to ask because she changed the subject. Giving Lucan a pat to let him know she was done with his back, Ilyssa stood and went to our supply pack. "Let's eat and get moving," she urged, which was what we did.

Three gray mountains were grim as their description. They stood in a line, ashen and bleak, with balding patches and stunted trees. I could see why Mellora's people thought such mountains were dying.

After we flew through a pass to the far side of the first sagging peak, we discovered a bowl-like hollow so strange it looked like a wound. We stopped, each of us perched in a different spindly tree overlooking the basin where the soil was stained orange, brown, yellow or green.

Mud pots burped up bubbles. Steam shot out of the ground to lie in slicks of blistered water, but those things weren't what held our attention. There were holes in the mountainside, and several buildings set in the hollow, the largest two flanking a huge barrel standing on wooden legs. Shacks only twice as wide as a man were scattered over much of the basin's bottom. Each had a vent in the top with steam coming from it. Some of the shack doors stood open, revealing men bent over pots or benches. Beyond the shacks, an empty corral, wheel ruts and a broken cart showed that caravans had visited in the past. A footpath led to a dark, yawning cavern on the far side of the basin.

Ilyssa pointed toward a clump of pines. Four of these had been tied together at the top. A net stretched over the dome they made. Beside the tree, a man with a levered crossbow like the ones caravan guards used was sprawled on the ground. I was surprised to see he was a falco like me.

"Oresmiths?" I mouthed silently to Lucan.

"What else?" he whispered. "That one's guarding something, but I can't make out what's under the netting."

I frowned. The pandion's warning about oresmiths made me want to avoid them. I waved a retreat toward thicker trees behind the crusty lip of the basin. We gathered in the shade of firs to discuss our next move.

"If we leave those oresmiths alone, why should they bother us?" Mellora reasoned. "I say we just go around them."

Chip was holding out his necklace, turning slowly in place. His hand jerked toward the bowl. He looked excited as he rumbled and pointed.

"The cavern?" Lucan asked him very slowly. "You want to go there?"

Chip nodded vigorously.

"Great," I muttered, "just great. Wouldn't you know that we have to get past the oresmiths to look for Chip's rainbow stone."

"If we wait until dark, the oresmiths might think we're Chiros and ignore us. There have to be lots of Chiros around that cavern," Lucan said.

"How right you are," a sullen, male voice drawled just before a net dropped over us. We struggled against the lines, but the net held. We were surrounded by Chiros.

I'd never seen one close up, and viewing a mob of them through netting didn't improve their looks. These had grey-brown skin and matching, featherless wings with hooked claws on the folds. Their ribbed ears covered the sides of their heads from jaw to reddish furred crown. Snub noses, thin lips, and solid black eyes made their expressions hard to read. This bunch had orange paint smeared on their faces and chests. For clothing, they wore only short, leather breeches.

I counted five Chiros. Two held the net while two others pointed spears. The fifth, a thin, young one who acted like a leader, circled us. When he got to Chip, he moved closer, peering into the net until their faces were only a hand's width apart. He touched Chip's head. Chip shrank away, mumbling something, but the Chiro didn't react to the sound. He moved on until he got to Ilyssa, who was next to me.

"Tropical female," he noted, "with no escort caravan?" Next, he shocked us all by talking to Ilyssa in the language Tropicals speak with each other.

Ilyssa gaped at him. He repeated the sounds, and she responded haltingly.

"You're out of practice," the Chiro said critically in ordinary words, "or you can't believe you're having a conversation with a *beast*."

"Where did you learn to speak Tropical?" Ilyssa asked.

"In the great city of Ladana where I was a slave," the Chiro snarled, raising his hand for silence. "Enough talk." He turned to his men. "Release them. If anyone gives you trouble, slice off his flight feathers."

The net lifted away, and I felt a spear prod my side. "Move," a lanky, tall guy ordered, pointing us toward a downhill trail.

"Wait!" I said. "I have a friendship gift from Chiros."

"Show it." The leader watched me closely while I searched in our supply pack for the clay circle my mother gave me. I held it up to him.

He snorted. "You taunt me with a symbol of our enemies? That's the coast tribe's emblem." He drew his shoulders back. "We are *mountain* Chiros." Lifting his head in a quick signal to his men, the leader resumed the march, and I got jabbed with the spear again.

Hopeless now, I fell into step next to Ilyssa. She took my hand, whether to comfort herself or me, I didn't know. Any other time, I'd have been thrilled; just then, I was too worried to enjoy it.

Behind us, Mellora asked, "What if we call out to the oresmiths?"

"Then you ruin our plan, and we don't need you anymore," the leader warned over his shoulder.

Chip rumbled something to Lucan, who replied, "I don't know."

The leader stopped and turned. "Why are you talking?"

"I'm answering my friend."

"That one speaks?" the leader asked, surprised.

"Of course." Lucan nudged Chip, urging him to, "Say something."

Chip squeezed his throat and choked out, "Yesss."

The leader tapped his ear. "I hear nothing."

"He said 'yes,'" Lucan reported.

The leader scrutinized Chip. "He has fur and strange wings. Ask him if he is part Chiro."

Lucan did that and Chip shook his head. The leader turned away.

"Stop!" Ilyssa commanded. "I insist you tell us where we're going. What do you want from us?" When a spear poked her, Ilyssa yelped.

I pulled her inside my wings. "Leave her alone!" I barked.

"Silence," the leader commanded, "or lose your flight feathers and *walk* everywhere until they grow again."

Ilyssa shrugged free of me. She told the leader hotly, "You won't get away with kidnapping us. My father's an important man. You just wait until Aurelius Too hears about—"

The leader's back went rigid and he spun around, demanding, "You know Honorable Too?"

"He's my father," Ilyssa said proudly, crossing her arms and tapping a foot for emphasis.

The leader put his face up to hers, scowling fiercely. Then he threw back his head and spit out sharp laughter. "That man was my slave master in Ladana."

"That's crazy," Ilyssa seethed. "My father doesn't keep slaves."

"You're right," the Chiro said, chortling now. "He freed me." Issuing a series of rapid clicks to the other Chiros, the leader nodded as they lowered their spears. He seized Ilyssa's hand, saying, "I am Rafik. You know of Rafik?"

She looked at the ground, her lips pursed, and then stared into his face. "I remember something of a Chiro won from a bet on a coleo race."

"Yes, yes. That is me—Rafik!" The leader grinned and pounded his chest.

"So…we're friends now?" I ventured. "I mean you and Miss Too are friends?"

Rafik clicked to his men. They and their net disappeared into the trees. "It's too early to be up," he remarked, yawning. "They should have rest before tonight, but we must talk. Come." He indicated a jumble of rough boulders, waving us into their shade. After we'd settled, he asked, "Why are you here?"

"We need a stone from the cavern," Lucan told him.

"You've come to rob us, just like the oresmiths," Rafik concluded, his voice going cold.

"We only want one stone, and we'll trade whatever we have for it," Ilyssa promised.

"What sort of stone? What trade goods do you offer?"

Lucan motioned to Chip to produce his necklace. Rafik drew back, averting his eyes, spreading his clawed fingertips wide. "That stone is forbidden to all but a shaman."

"Chip is a shaman," I said, thinking that *might* be true. We didn't know he wasn't. "He already has one stone, but he needs another."

Rafik mulled this over. "If you speak truth, then our goals are the same, for only a shaman may lead another shaman to the place of rainbow stones. Our shaman, Kalmus, is a captive of the oresmiths, held in that tree prison they made. If you help us free him, he might take your shaman to the stones."

"I don't understand," Ilyssa said. "Why do the oresmiths want your shaman?"

"He knows the mountain better than anyone else. The oresmiths force him to show them where metals can be found, and with Kalmus is in their hands, we dare not attack them."

"But when we showed up, you thought you could work out a trade," I realized.

Rafik shrugged. "Strangers do not come here any longer. Friends to oresmiths could have value to them."

"Not us," Lucan put in. "The oresmiths don't know us. They'd think we came to steal their metal or their secrets, and imprison us, too. That wouldn't help anyone."

Rafik leaned on a fist. He eyed Mellora.

"Don't even *think* of trading her for your shaman." Grasping for a reason he might accept, I added, "She's Miss Too's servant. Honorable Too would be furious."

"I was considering her color," Rafik explained. "She has much white in her plumage—easy to see at night—and she would be a suitable distraction during a raid on the prison."

"I could…" Mellora began, but Ilyssa silenced her with a glance and said, "We're not going to risk Mellora or anyone else."

"No," I said slowly, remembering how Thomis the Shore had told me that protecting all his people was the most important thing. "There's a better way to get to Kalmus. We just have to become invisible."

CHAPTER FIFTEEN

River of Light

After dark, the Chiros' shaman would be awake, but the oresmiths would be ending their day. They'd change guards around the supper hour, I figured.

Rafik said I was right. "Unless they take Kalmus from the tree prison to lead them to metal, he will be fed when the night guard comes out to replace the day guard."

"Can you speak to him with those clicks you use?" Lucan asked. "It'll be easier if Kalmus knows what's happening."

Lucan, who would have the biggest part to play in the plan, was growing jittery from waiting. He barely touched his meal and preened restlessly. In the light of the nearly full moon, his dark skin and feathers would merge into the deep moon shadows so he could sneak up to the prison tree and cut the net around Kalmus, but twilight still lingered in the sky.

We were counting on Lucan and his firestone knife. Rafik's spear blade was made of ordinary, rough stone. With so many oresmiths forging tools, Ilyssa had asked why the Chiros had no metal knives or spear tips. "They give you nothing?"

"Nothing but trouble," Rafik said bitterly. "When the first ones arrived, they were few but we were many. We let them gather ore and work their metal because they left us alone. Then more of them came.

They grew bold, forcing their way into our home cavern and treating us as beasts.

"As an orphaned pup, I crept from the cavern, desperate for food. An oresmith captured me and sold me to a caravan going south to Ladana. There I went to coleo trainers who used me to tend their stock at night."

I shared a look with Ilyssa. We agreed silently *not* to ask if Chaya's family had been those coleo trainers. While Ilyssa murmured her sympathies, I concentrated on making the fine netting Thomis gave us resemble the ground around the tree prison. Though I had to guess what was there, I thought I'd done a good job of adding pine needles to dry leaves and sticking them onto the net with a muddy paste made from water, soil and clay. My disguise didn't have to be perfect. I only needed it until I got close enough to rush the night guard and put him to sleep.

We'd thought for a long time about what to do with the guard. No one except Rafik felt right about killing him, so we'd been stuck on that point until Rafik reminded us that fumes from some of the steaming holes made people dizzy and weak. The Chiros couldn't capture the fumes, but Chip's mask could. To our surprise, he still had this; he'd kept it in a space within his wings. Chip told Lucan (who told Rafik, who told one of his men) how to make the mask pull in fumes. At first, Rafik's man was afraid of Chip and terrified of handling our shaman's "magic" mask, but he finally went to a distant mud pot and carefully filled the box attached to the mask. Chip showed me how to make the box send fumes into the mask. Now all I had to do was get the mask on the night guard.

I was nearly as nervous as Lucan because this was *my* plan, and if it didn't work, it would be my fault. Pacing around the rocks outside the basin, I checked again to make sure everyone could pass by the oresmiths unnoticed. Chip was fine in his brown suit and face paint, but

Mellora's light feathers had to be covered completely by the wraps my mother gave us. Ilyssa wore her cloak. The hood was loose, leaving the tip of one crest feather visible. Tucking this in and tying the string tightly under her chin, I studied her. She had missed painting a spot just above her mouth. As I smoothed the paint with my finger, Ilyssa looked at me with trusting eyes. I felt her breath warm on my face. Her lips looked soft. Suddenly, I had the impulse to kiss her—me, Kor Tiercel.

I was out of my mind.

Shaking my head, I turned back to Rafik, who informed me his men were in place around the basin. They would pretend to go out hunting as always, providing cover for Ilyssa, Mellora and Chip to slip into the Chiros' cavern. With the three of them safely inside, Lucan and I could sneak up on the guard, daze him with the mask, and get Kalmus. The other Chiros would wait until Kalmus was free. After that, what they did depended on the oresmiths.

It was time. As I covered myself with the Shores' net, I realized that while we helped the Chiros with their problem, the Mountaineers were helping our grove. It was like a big circle taking us all in. I had to believe the gods were behind this somehow, and that thought gave me courage.

S hivering from cold wind and from nerves, Lucan and I stood behind trees at the basin's rim. Our friends had gone with Rafik toward the cavern. We couldn't see them, and that was a good thing.

Below us, light was coming from the largest oresmith building. Whenever the door opened loud talk and laughter spilled out, the sounds men make when they're drinking wine. Oresmiths went back and forth from a shack that was probably their latrine. I'd expected that.

Chiros began flying out of their cavern, circling upward from the cave's mouth. Dark shapes filled the sky overhead. I had no idea there were so many Chiros. Seeing their numbers made me feel better.

Lucan watched the way they flew so he could look more like them. His wings weren't pointed, but he hoped to copy the Chiros' flight pattern. After a minute, we both knew how foolish that idea was. On the upstroke, Chiros folded their wings tight to their bodies, shooting forward because there was no drag. They could reverse direction in a space less than half their wingspan. Compared to them, we were clumsy and slow.

"At least I can dip and rise," Lucan muttered, "and zigzag. They don't fly straight lines like we do."

Nodding agreement, I started toward the basin. I had to knock out the guard before Lucan cut the net, so I stole behind the next tree. For a while, I could stay hidden, but the trees thinned near the bottom of the slope. I'd be in the open for a long way, waiting to move only when the guard's head was turned.

It took a lifetime to creep down that hill, every gain making my heart beat faster. I saw Lucan fly by, bobbing up and down like a Chiro. The only reason I spotted him was because I was looking for him. He perched on a slender pine two wing beats from the prison tree as I closed in from the other direction.

What happened next was *not* my fault. The mountain shook, making me stumble just as the guard did a small jig of his own. After the tremor stopped, his head snapped sharply in my direction, and I knew he'd seen me. He called out. When I didn't answer, he raised his bow and shot an arrow.

I twisted sideways. The arrow caught my net disguise, ripping it away. I was completely exposed to the next arrow, already being nocked.

Then the guard went down, clipped at the knees by Chip, who shouldn't have been there. He was supposed to be safe in the cavern. When I rushed over with the mask, I was glad for his help. Though the guard yelled and struggled, Chip's strong arms held him until he slumped into sleep. I pulled off the mask.

All this happened fast, but the guard's cries had been so loud, I knew everyone in the basin heard him. Sure enough, the door to the big hall banged open and men scrambled out.

"Hurry!" I yelled to Lucan, who sawed at the net. In seconds, the oresmiths would be on us.

"Can't...get...the...last...strand," Lucan gritted out through his teeth. Inside the prison, Kalmus, an aged Chiro, tugged at the ropes until his wiry arm muscles knotted. He clicked to his people overhead.

The noise grew frighteningly loud as thousands of Chiros joined in. It was a fearsome sound, an angry buzzing that stopped most of the oresmiths in their tracks. They peered upward, knowing they had no chance against so many. Sensible oresmiths shoved each other to get back to the safety of their hall, but a rowdy few started shouting insults. They soon found themselves targeted by rings of spears.

With a mighty yank on the net of the prison tree, Chip tore an opening big enough for Kalmus to climb through. The shaman eyed Chip's rainbow stone, which was hanging outside his garment. Kalmus touched a clawed finger to the stone, fired off a stream of clicks, and then gripped Chip's left hand, pulling him near so their forearms were locked against each other with fists upraised. "Pull," Kalmus hissed, shutting his eyes. "Pull down the sky."

Chip stared at him. So did I.

Kalmus groaned and opened his eyes. "More spirit," he said, seizing my right hand as he had Chip's, linking the three of us together.

Overhead, clear green light poured down. I had seen colored lights in the sky before, but never this wide, bright river that flowed above us, serene and sure, filling me with awe and taking my fear away. I felt as though I were drifting comfortably in some peaceful, timeless place, completely at ease. When the light thinned and rippled away, the entire basin was silent. The last of the oresmiths staggered into their hall, and it was over.

Kalmus released Chip and me, smiled pleasantly to Lucan, and dipped his round, white-furred head to each of us. We fell into step behind him along the footpath to the cavern. None of us boys said anything about the light; we didn't even look at each other. We'd just seen magic. There were no words.

Then a crowd of excited, clicking Chiros surrounded us, obviously thrilled to have their shaman back. When Rafik plowed through the throng, I found my voice again. I asked him about the oresmiths and what they might do next. Would they get weapons and come to attack the cavern? Rafik shrugged, unconcerned. Kalmus was free, which was all that mattered. If the oresmiths wanted a fight, they would get one.

Ilyssa and Mellora ran up to inspect us, asking if we were all right and chattering with relief. The girls told us that the cavern was wonderful, which we saw for ourselves, once we passed through the great cave mouth and a long tube passageway beyond this. Unlike the dark, closed-in places I'd imagined Chiro caves to be, we found an enormous space with massive, colorful pillars thrusting up from the floor or hanging from the ceiling like frozen water. We could see all this because glowworms seemed to be everywhere along the walls.

Little Chiros pointed and hid behind their mothers when Ilyssa took off her cloak. They'd probably never seen a Tropical before. Ilyssa smiled and waved them to come to her, which the bolder ones did, even stretching curious hands to stroke her white feathers. By the time we settled onto rocks in the great cavern, Ilyssa had a circle of little ones around her.

Kalmus took Chip to the place of the rainbow stones. I was content to wait for them, watching the Chiros dance and sing as they celebrated their shaman's return. Though the sounds were odd—more like a droning hum than singing—the joyful feeling drew me in just the same. Still, I was getting tired, only too ready for sleep when Chip returned, beaming with satisfaction and holding out a stone that filled his palm.

Rafik led us to a side chamber we could use for sleep. There we found hammocks strung near the ceiling and our supply bag, which the Chiros had brought in for us. Without the claws Chiros used to move around on the rocks, we knew it would be difficult to reach the hammocks, but after washing off our face paint in a pool of water, we tackled the climb and then rolled into the nets, nearly body to body. I didn't mind; Ilyssa was next to me. When she complained of being cold, I stretched my wing over her and lay awake until she slept.

CHAPTER SIXTEEN

Vala, the Cloud Mountain

I opened my eyes to a mouth of pointed teeth hanging over me. I screeched.

Rafik grinned and dropped from the ceiling to sprawl on the ledge near my hammock. His face turned serious. "Dawn approaches. You must go before the oresmiths awaken."

"Go where?"

"To the Cloud Mountain. Kalmus says that place holds your destiny."

That didn't sound right. "I have a *destiny*?"

"Your destiny is to help your shaman," Rafik told me, pointing toward Chip.

"Oh. Oh, yeah," I said, relieved.

My yell and the talking woke Ilyssa. She looked at my wing, still stretched over her and murmured, "I was warm last night." The soft look on her face made me happy. But then it was gone, so I pulled in my wing. "Do you mean Vala, the mountain with the Cave of the Gods?" Ilyssa asked Rafik. "It's not far from here."

"This mountain is home to pale spirits," Rafik replied. "They call the clouds to shade them from the sun."

"Vala's clouds are like that," Ilyssa recalled. "They curve over the peak and stay there instead of floating away." She turned to me. "I'm sure Rafik means Vala, but I hope we don't have to go to the top. The

Cave of the Gods is only part-way up, and it's hard to breathe even there."

"You have your shaman's magic mask. Will that not help?" Rafik asked.

Lucan, who'd been listening to this conversation, nudged Chip awake. As Chip rubbed his eyes, Lucan asked about the mask. Chip rumbled at Lucan, who told us, "He says he can change the mask to hold air from the base of the mountain. We can take breaths from that. He wonders how Kalmus knows what we should do, since Kalmus couldn't hear him when he talked."

Rafik looked surprised. "Kalmus is Kalmus."

So, taking the Chiro shaman's advice, we found ourselves standing inside the cave's mouth as the sun rose. "Are you sure we shouldn't stay to help if the oresmiths come to attack you?" Lucan asked.

Rafik swept one hand in an arc. Dozens of Chiro men emerged from the shadows. He waved them back into their positions of watchful waiting.

"You have done enough," Rafik told Lucan, and he handed him a clay circle. "Every mountain Chiro will call you friend. These stones," he told Ilyssa and Mellora, giving each nuggets of gleaming ore, "will add to your bride prices. For you, there is this." Rafik thrust a leather bag into my hand.

I pulled on the drawstring. "This is a rainbow stone. You said only shamans were allowed to have these."

"Kalmus said it is for you."

"But—"

"Kalmus is never wrong."

We left the basin without meeting any oresmiths. I was glad for that but sad we didn't know what would happen to our new friends. Some things, I guess, must be left to the gods. I hoped they'd take care of the Chiros.

Once we passed beyond the gray mountains, the towering, snow-covered peak of Vala stood between us and the sea. There were other ridges around it, but these were low compared to the great, pointed cone of the Cloud Mountain. When he saw it, Chip pounded his chest. Clearly, he wanted to go there.

I was uneasy about the mountain. Woodlanders knew Vala was home to spirits long before the Grays arrived to tell us about the Cave of the Gods. We thought the spirits were friendly and wanted to help us. After a long winter, my people would bring gifts to thank the spirits for the return of spring. When the Grays told us the spirits were gods who did not want us to visit, that the clouds curving down like a frown were a warning to stay away, we were surprised, but we listened to the Tropical priests and left Vala alone except during Summit Flights, when the Grays said the best of our young wings were welcome at the Cave.

The mountain grew larger as we flew toward it. We reached its foothills by late morning. There we ate, in a valley where the trees rustled with red and yellow leaves though it was winter at the top of the mountain. How could this be so—winter beside autumn? What other secrets did Vala hold?

No one but Chip seemed eager to move forward. He busied himself with his mask, opening parts and closing others. I wasn't sure how the mask could make us less tired, which was why Ilyssa had struggled during her Summit Flight, I thought. Whenever a person exercises too long, he gasps for breath, and yet no one carries around a mask.

Lucan looked more strained than he had before our raid on the tree prison. His face was pinched and his eyes narrowed every time he looked up at Vala. Mellora asked him what was wrong. Lucan told her, "It's not time for a Summit Flight. The gods don't want us on the mountain. The Grays say we'll make the gods angry."

"I don't trust the Grays," Ilyssa declared. "They didn't know anything about Chip. They wanted to kill him. I say they're the ones who are wrong."

"But if they're not," Lucan persisted, "we could be cursed. What if…what if Chip has to live in the sky now because he angered the gods? What if he was like us until the gods changed him?"

"If the gods changed Chip, then they can change him back," I said. "You're just the person to tell them to do that. You're the only one who's likely to understand what they say."

Chip squeezed his throat and said, "Yesss."

Lucan sighed, then punched Chip's shoulder. "You're not going to let me out of this, are you?"

Chip grinned and tapped his fingers together in the gesture that meant Lucan. Lucan smiled thinly, but after that, he was ready to go on.

The Cave of the Gods, Ilyssa explained, wasn't at the top of the mountain but more to one side, its opening half-ringed by rocks. Ilyssa urged us to take wing because the clouds would close in by noon, and without direct sunlight, we would feel colder.

Leaving our supply pack in the valley, we began our ascent. The mountain was so broad that our flight would be long but not steep. Ilyssa began shivering soon after we took off, and yet she kept on flying with a determined look on her face and fast, strong beats of her wings.

I pictured her on the Summit Flight last year and realized how much harder fighting the chilly mountain wind had been for her, a Tropical, than for a Woodlander. It was a humbling thought.

It was humbling, too, to find myself short of breath only part-way up the mountain. Though I wasn't tired, no matter how hard I sucked in air, I wanted more. The others had landed on the slope, where they were breathing through Chip's mask. The only one who didn't need the mask was Chip. His breathing was easy, and he looked more comfortable than he'd been all the while we'd traveled together. After I took a turn with the mask, the flying was better.

On the mountainside below, animals with white fur leapt across the rocks. They had small horns but no other defense against coleos or myrmecs that I could see. I guessed they didn't need them here, surrounded by snow. This was truly a strange place.

I flew alongside Mellora, who seemed entirely relaxed and content. She'd come from the ice lands, so maybe the mountain reminded her of home. Smiling and waving to me, she pointed out more of the white animals from time to time before the shadow fell over us both.

In the next seconds, so many things happened, they take longer to describe than they took to live. Mellora and I looked up to find the source of the shadow. I saw something I'd feared since I was downy: a molluk. Three times my size, it could be nothing else.

If molluks were hungry enough, they'd eat any kind of meat, even from people. They didn't make clean kills but wounded prey by breaking wings or limbs, and then they waited for the victim to die. Sometimes, they didn't wait that long. While still a nestling, I'd seen a molluk tear into a sea animal stranded on the beach by Sea Grove. After that, visions of wrinkled, red heads and black wings with the white linings filled my nightmares.

Mellora yelled to me, "Protect the mistress. I will draw him away."

"No!"

"Trust me. I can do this. Do not follow!" Mellora shouted before dropping sharply downward with a bent wing.

Of course, I went after her, but the molluk got between us. Mellora fell in a patch of loose snow, rolling until she clambered into a crevice between rocks. The molluk landed to paw at the ground. He was too big to reach Mellora inside the narrow cleft.

I rose up to dive on him, but he'd seen me. He lifted off to face me down, flapping his giant wings in challenge. I hovered, uncertain what to do until I saw two more molluks coming at us.

As the first molluk went to defend his prize against the would-be poachers, I heard Mellora call out, "Kor, go. Go *now*."

May the gods forgive me, I did.

"**Y**ou *left* her?" Ilyssa raged. She tried to slap me, but I caught her arm and pulled her back behind the rocks where the others had hidden when they saw the molluks. Beating on my hand, she howled, "Let go of me, you coward. I'll rescue her myself!"

"I didn't tell you the rest," I hissed. "She escaped."

"How do you know that?"

"I saw her sneaking away after the molluks started fighting."

Ilyssa spat out, "Why didn't you say so in the first place?"

I bellowed into her face, "You didn't give me a chance!"

Chip waved both hands at us. It didn't take Lucan to explain that. Chip wanted us to shut up. I sat down to wait, my back to Ilyssa. All of us took turns breathing from Chip's mask.

The clouds closed over the mountain and the breeze picked up, sending swirls of snow spiraling on the gusts. Mellora took advantage of these. We barely caught sight of her before she reached us, to be hugged fiercely by Ilyssa.

"I am fine, Mistress," Mellora assured her. Setting Ilyssa aside, Mellora shook snow from her feathers. "I know how to trick molluks."

"But how did you get away?" Lucan asked.

"First, I hid among the rocks, then tunneled through snow, and finally stayed in the shadow of trees until the molluks forgot about me. Molluks are stupid. They are much easier to fool than Tundran hunters. Sometimes," Mellora added, "we phasians have to dive into snow banks to escape hunters and hide, not moving at all, until they go away."

"How can you stand the cold?" Ilyssa asked, shivering with sympathy. She chafed at Mellora's arms. "You must be freezing."

"I could use a wrap," Mellora admitted.

Our pack was at the base of the mountain. I began to pull off my tunic. It wasn't much, but it was better than nothing.

Mellora shook her head. "Your arms and wings around me," she said with a smile, "will be enough."

It was no trouble to warm Mellora that way. No trouble at all.

We were just below the entrance to the Cave of the Gods, Ilyssa told us. With a withering glance in my direction, she said we should move on before the day got later.

I don't know what I expected from the Cave—huge, scowling statues? A chorus of singing spirits? The entrance rocks looked like all the others on the mountain. The only difference was a smooth ice tunnel leading into the darkness. That was it. I was disappointed.

Lucan was thrilled. He said, "There aren't any warnings from the gods. All we have to do is go in."

"A way that looks so easy," Mellora said, "can be a trap. Mistress, is this entrance as you remember it?"

Ilyssa held the back of her hand to her forehead as she peered at the tunnel. "There was a flag…bright green. I was ahead of the others, but some were close behind me. I could only think of the flag, and how I wanted to reach it first. That's all I remember until I woke up inside."

I asked Lucan, "Could whatever Chip needs be outside the Cave?"

Chip didn't wait for Lucan to translate. He reached a hand across himself to touch a place high on his wings. Points of light appeared along the leading edges. Jerking his chin toward us, Chip turned and entered the darkness.

CHAPTER SEVENTEEN

Cave of the Gods

We followed Chip into the ice tunnel. It ended at a stone wall with a wooden door. The door had a metal box and a bar that stuck into the rock. The box had symbols on it. Chip stroked these with a fingernail, making the symbols turn. We heard a click, and the bar slid behind the box. Chip pulled the door open to lead us into the Cave of the Gods.

From the echoing sounds our footsteps made on the stone floor, I guessed that the cave was high and wide. We had only the light from Chip's wings, so we couldn't see much beyond a bench by the door that had a rack of masks on it. Each mask was attached to a rubber hose, and that led to a box on wheels. There was a leather strap on the back of each box.

Ilyssa stared at the masks for a moment, and then reached for one. Chip shook his head when she offered it to him. Ilyssa handed the rest of us masks and showed us how to put them over our noses, then tie the ends behind our heads. She pushed on the top of my box, and I felt wind flowing into my nose. It smelled like air from the base of the mountain. The mask didn't cover my mouth, so I could have talked if I'd wanted to. Standing there in the scary darkness, I didn't have anything to say.

Next, Ilyssa pulled on a rope beside the door. I heard a creaking sound, and then sunlight shone down through a hole that opened near the ceiling of the cave. A shower of snow fell in before a sheet of clear stuff like Chip had on his mask closed the hole. Metal wheels somewhere clanked. The shape of the hole changed, and sunlight struck a shiny circle by the far wall, bouncing off it to strike another circle, and then another, until we were surrounded by light.

Lucan said, "I don't understand. Where are the gods? This looks like a workshop."

It did. Along the walls stood more benches with wood, clay, or metal objects, and stools set out before them. Some things I recognized, like bowls and hammers, but other shapes were complicated and strange. There were shelves filled with baskets, and tall boxes with doors. Wood panels marked with curving Tropical script were nailed to posts attached to the benches. When I asked Ilyssa to read these, she said there were no words, only letters, numbers, and symbols.

Ilyssa walked beside the benches, pulling her box along as we went. She trailed the fingertips of her right hand on the dusty surfaces, and then stopped to pick up a metal tool. After studying this for a moment, she laid it down and said, "I didn't remember any of this until now. I remembered the Summit Flight, gasping for breath, and the mask on my face when I woke. But the rest...." She turned in place, looking around the cavern. "I spent one week here, and the days passed like a dream. When it was time to fly home, a Gray talked to me. He waved something in front of my eyes, and the next thing I knew, I was back at the knoll. Since then, an idea or word will come into my head, but I don't understand what it means."

Near the back wall, a cloudy shape started forming. It took on the outline of a man wearing a garment that was white near his face and gray everywhere else. His head was smooth as a molluk's. There were no arches of wings behind his shoulders.

Was this a god? I wanted to run away, but I stood there, frozen by fear. When the shape began to grumble, my heart jumped into my throat, and I thought my life was over.

Chip rattled off a long stream of rumbling sounds that made Lucan's eyebrows go up.

"What?" I whispered.

"Chip says the cloud man is not alive. It is only a picture."

"But he moves...and speaks."

Rubbing her forehead, Ilyssa squinted at the thing and then said, "Chip's right. I saw this vision when I was here before. There's a way to make it clearer." Going to a spot just in front of the wavering cloud, she tapped her foot on a metal plate set in the floor. The god or vision— I didn't know what to call him—stopped. After a pause, he began moving and talking faster. Suddenly, I could understand him. I heard these words:

> Greetings. Do not be afraid. You are in no danger. You're seeing an image of me from far, far away. My name is Dr. Gene Ormond.

"Geen!" Lucan cried, rushing to the metal plate to make the words stop. "It's the god Geen." He stared at Chip.

Chip shook his head. He spoke to Lucan, then stood by the metal plate.

"Not a god," Lucan translated. "Just one of Chip's people. Chip says to listen to the rest." Lucan nodded to Chip, who touched the plate.

> I am a human man from a place called Earth. Long ago, my kind learned how to send messengers across great distances. The messengers are not alive. They are tools, like the arrows and

spears your people make, but they are not for hunting. One of these messengers is in the sky above you. Our messengers send sounds that can be heard in special places of your world where minerals strengthen those sounds. Now, we have the ability to hear what you say, but it takes two of your moons for each message to travel back and forth.

Over time, we learned that only growing, young minds could absorb the information we sent. A boy named Lissan was the first to understand our words. He founded the Order of Gray. Throughout many of your generations, the Order has selected youths of the right age to follow our instructions. We taught those individuals to build all that you see around you for one purpose: to receive the first human visitor to your land. If you are here to help in this important work, we thank you.

The cloud faded. I stood stunned, staring at the place where it had been. When I turned to Chip, he was looking at a red, blinking light on the floor. He bent to press the red spot, then stepped back when the cloud man reappeared.

Ormand here. This is an emergency message to any member of the Order of Gray. A dangerous situation is developing in our land. For the moment we are safe, but we cannot wait longer to send a human to your world. His task is to find a mineral natural to your planet but nearly impossible to create on ours. To make the tiny amount of this element he will use took years and vast resources. What he brings back will make long-distance travel possible for our people. So much depends on his success.

At this point, the cloud man's speech slowed, the pitch falling until it was so low the words no longer made sense. I asked Ilyssa, "Can you make him talk better?"

"Shh," Lucan hissed. "I want to hear more."

"You know what he's saying?" Mellora asked.

"Be quiet." Lucan cocked an ear toward the cloud man. "He's telling about...wait. I'll say the words out loud."

> We can only send and bring back one person. Our choice is Alexander Rasken, whose parents have been working on this project. They believe, as I do, that he is the right age to communicate with you. Alexander will have some trouble breathing your air because of its high oxygen content...

Lucan paused. "What?" Ilyssa asked.

"The man stopped talking. Oh, now he's starting again."

> I mean to say your air is too rich for our kind. High on the mountain it will be fine, but near sea level, it can make us feel ill. Alexander will have a mask to help with this problem, and we have given him artificial wings so he can travel as you do, but his wings will work only during daylight hours. We are hoping that they won't be affected adversely by your lower gravity.

> We are all concerned for Alexander's safety. I pray that you receive this message before he arrives so you can give him your help. Thank you. Ormond out.

The cloud disappeared again. Lucan said to Chip, "Allasander?"

He gripped his throat. "Yesss." Then he tapped his chest. "Chiiiip."

Ilyssa said slowly to Chip—I couldn't get used to thinking of him with a new name—"The Grays didn't get that message, did they? They didn't know you were coming or what you had to do. It must have been frightening for you to come here and find nobody."

Chip nodded, and Ilyssa went on. "So…so you went out looking for people, right? And you found Sea Grove, then Kor and me. We took you to the Grays. Why didn't they help you?"

"Because they expected a god," said Lucan, "not a boy with fur on his head. The cloud man doesn't have fur."

That was true. I asked why Chip was different.

Lucan listened to Chip's answer and reported, "He says the old ones of his kind sometimes molt, but their fur doesn't grow in again like our feathers do. All the young ones are furred, and—*What?*" Lucan asked Chip to repeat what he'd just said. After he did, Lucan looked doubtful, but he told us, "None of Chip's people has wings. They don't fly. They don't live in the clouds; they just travel that way. They move around on the *ground*, day and night."

No wonder there was trouble in his land! I thought about the terrible dangers people would face if they had to stay where insects could get at them all the time. I didn't want Chip to go back to that, and I said so.

Chip told Lucan the problem wasn't insects but people. Some of them were like our Tundrans: They wanted more territory. Then I understood he had to go back to help his people, just as we'd done for Sea Grove.

Mellora said what I was thinking. "So you must go home, Chip. Do you know how to do that?"

He pointed toward the place where the cloud man had been.

Ilyssa's eyes filled with tears. "Then this is goodbye." In an instant, she was embracing Chip and saying, "Please, please be careful."

Chip smiled and hugged us all, adding a long speech when he got to Lucan, who said, "The Summit Flights are the best time for us to talk to Chip's people. He wants me to be here for the next one." Lucan screwed up his face and said sourly, "As if a corvid forager could outfly everyone else!" A second later, he rubbed his lips thoughtfully. "Well, I do know the way, and I have until spring to come up with plan to get here first." Lucan asked Chip, "Say, can I have your mask?"

"Will there still be Summit Flights?" Ilyssa wondered as Chip handed Lucan the mask. "If we built this place so Chip could come to get what he needed, why should the flights continue?"

Chip rumbled to Lucan, who looked pleased by what he heard. "This is just the beginning. With the rainbow stone, more of his people can visit us. We have to get ready for them."

"What about the Grays?" Ilyssa countered. "What will happen when Sea Grove finds out there are no gods here? Will the Grays stop being so important? Maybe *that's* why they wanted to kill Chip—to keep things the way they've always been."

I looked at Ilyssa. Sometimes she was so smart, she was scary.

Lucan said, "We have to tell the Council of Elders what we've seen. After that, the Grays won't be able to hide the truth."

"Will Chip be back?" Mellora asked.

Chip held out both of his rainbow stones. He clinked them together. I didn't know what he meant.

"I think that's a yes," said Ilyssa. "We will be together again."

So, when Chip laid his stones and wings on the spot where the cloud man had been, I didn't feel sad. I watched him step onto the metal plate and stand tall. *This isn't goodbye forever*, I told myself. But as a bubble formed around him and disappeared with Chip inside waving to us all,

I had to gulp and blink a lot. Lucan swiped at his eyes.

Clinging to Mellora, Ilyssa cried openly, arguing with herself even as she sobbed. "Oh, I feel so foolish. I shouldn't be crying. He's going *home*. He'll be with his people, his family. I don't know why I'm crying." She went on that way for a while, then rubbed her face and was done.

I said, "It's time for us all to go home."

CHAPTER EIGHTEEN

Home

We paused outside the ice tunnel, searching the sky for molluks. It was late afternoon, so Mellora told us not to worry: Molluks rode thermals during the hottest part of the day. She must have been right, for we sailed down the mountain without crossing paths with any of the terrifying giants. The question after that was whether to stay inland or to travel along the coast? If there were a strong, onshore breeze, we'd have to fight against that, but if not, we'd get to Sea Grove sooner. Too impatient to take the longer, slower route, we made for the sea and home.

Home. I tried not to think about what we might find there, but I couldn't chase away the fear. A year or so ago, I'd heard my parents talking late one night. Father said it was better to fall in battle than to let Tundrans decide how you died. Mother agreed.

What if we'd sent the Mountaineers to Sea Grove too late? What if Tundrans ruled our grove now? We might not have a home.

We flew urgently and without any interest in what was around us. Once we reached the sea, we followed the coast, trusting the shoreline to guide us.

That was a mistake. While I was in the lead, we rounded a headland and spotted a horde of war-painted Tundrans directly in our path. I wheeled toward the trees and risked a roll too near the ground so I could check on the others. Lucan and Mellora saw me, but Ilyssa was looking seaward. I watched in horror as she flew on, unaware of the danger.

All I could think to do was fly to her. The speed I had when the Tundran chieftain pursued her came back to me, and I reached Ilyssa in a couple of heartbeats. She looked at me with a puzzled expression until she saw what was coming. I pointed up, and we both pulled hard to get the height advantage.

To our amazement, the monsters swept past below us, not even glancing our way. From our new, higher position, we could see why they were winging at top speed: Mountaineers pursued them. I saw Loran in the lead and then some faces from Sea Grove, but the most welcome sight was my father. He separated from the others and waved us to shore.

After a happy reunion on the beach, we asked each other, "Are you all right?" He was, and so was my mother, who was off hunting.

"Food stocks at the grove are low," my father explained, "and she lost too many feathers in skirmishes to risk more combat." Adom was staying at the Mountaineers' camp, but he and Jass told my parents and the Elders about our travels, so Father knew much of what we'd done.

"My family?" Ilyssa asked fearfully.

No Tropicals had died, but their knoll took a heavy beating because raiders used their large roofs for cover. There'd been no corvid losses, either, Father assured Lucan. Deaths among hunters included people I knew, even one of the Elders.

"What ended the siege?" Mellora asked.

"We kept the Tundrans busy fighting at night, and they got no rest by day in their camp, which was attacked repeatedly by insects, thanks to a Stillwater who made a batch of stuff to attract every coleo and myrmec for miles."

"His name wouldn't be Brant, would it?" I asked.

"It is," said my father. "The Shore folk found him inside Tundran-controlled territory and helped him get home. In return, he cooked up brews to drive the Tundrans crazy.

"Then the Mountaineers arrived, and that was the last straw for the Tundrans. Their main group fled north this morning, though it took us until afternoon to roust out the stragglers. The fighting's over for now, but the rebuilding will take time.

"Your father," he told Ilyssa, "organized the resistance at your knoll and has plans to improve our grove's defenses. He's a good man to have on our side."

Father realized Chip wasn't with us. "What became of that furred boy?"

The four of us young wings looked at each other, not knowing where to begin. "He went home," I said finally. After the others nodded their agreement, I promised, "Tomorrow, we'll tell you and the Council about Chip and his people."

The nets were still up over Sea Grove, so we had to enter through the seaside gates. We passed a mound of dead Tundrans on a makeshift raft set on the sandbar. I asked one of the gate sentries about this.

"When the tide goes out, the Shores will haul the raft to deep water and sink it," she said. "If you ask me, that's too good for that Tundran scum. *I'd* leave the bodies for the molluks."

Father was called away to attend to something or other almost immediately. Everyone seemed busy, so we followed our noses to a food service area that had been set up during the siege and was still working. The cooks were serving both Tropical and Woodlander foods, and we were all starving, so we settled down at a long table.

We didn't talk much. Lucan was missing Chip, I think. Then Jass turned up, full of questions I was too tired to answer. Ilyssa didn't look like she was eager for conversation, either. Mellora saved us from Jass by promising to tell him everything if he'd leave the rest of us alone. She dragged him to the other end of the table.

Ilyssa ate quickly because she wanted to see her family. I offered to go with her, and she said I could. We waved goodbye to the others and went off on foot, having done enough flying for one day. Ilyssa held my arm, which was nice, but made me feel sad. After this walk, I'd probably never see her again, except in passing, when she might nod hello to me.

All around the grove, people repaired damage from the siege. Woodlanders took the lead, but I noticed that instead of just standing back giving orders, Tropicals pitched in, too. There were a lot of jokes flying around. Most people seemed in good spirits. There'd be mourning when we buried our dead, but for now, the people of Sea Grove were happy to be alive.

Watching a Tropical throw cracked pikes from the grounder stockade onto a pile, Ilyssa said to me, "Things will never be quite the same here, will they?" I agreed, but thought to myself that some things would be. After a while, Tropicals and Woodlanders would remember who they were—and who they weren't.

When we reached the knoll, we saw that the highest bridge between the Toos' tree and the tree beside it was gone. The villa's front landing platform held heaped debris. This had come from a Tropical nest, most of which lay shattered on the forest floor. "Oh, no!" said Ilyssa. "I hope our neighbors weren't there when it fell."

I hoped so, too. There wasn't much left of their home.

Ilyssa and I flew over the wreckage and then up to the platform behind the Toos' villa. The back gate hung from one hinge. Ferns near the path were trampled flat; the moss was torn off. Parts of broken branches littered the ground, some of these big enough to block our way so we had to climb over them.

We weren't looking ahead. When we saw him, Ilyssa jumped. Standing there watching us was Boran, the Mountaineer scat who'd nearly gotten Adom killed. Without the fancy tournament outfit, Boran looked like an ordinary Woodlander—a really big, ordinary Woodlander. Just then, I didn't care how big he was.

"Hey!" I shouted. "I still owe you one for my brother."

Boran curled his lip. "The little snitch couldn't take a joke. It's his fault I'm in disgrace."

I stepped toward him, my fists clenched.

Ilyssa caught my arm. "Kor, don't. He's not worth fighting. Last time I saw him, he was cleaning latrines. He—" She leaned forward to peer at a sack Boran was carrying. "That's Mellora's bag. She uses it when we go to shop from the caravans. What's *he* doing with it?"

"He's been doing his shopping from the knoll—from your villa," I growled. "The bag's full of stuff."

"Give me that." Ilyssa thrust out her hand. Boran shoved her away, and she fell.

Arrrrrr! I snapped my wings tight behind my back and swung at him. He blocked with his left arm and followed up with a right punch. I ducked, but he caught my jaw with a left upper cut. When I staggered back, Boran got just enough time to spin around and sprint up the path toward the pool.

I don't know what he was thinking as he took wing. The nets were still covering the grove. He wouldn't get away from me in the sky. I launched myself at him, catching the bag dangling from his hand, ripping it loose as I pulled him around.

Now *I* had a problem: His longer legs and arms kept me from closing in. As we circled above the ground, he'd shoot out a fist or foot, and the best I could do was dodge it. I couldn't get near enough to land a solid blow.

Then I remembered the move the Mountaineer girl made when she fought the aquilan in the tournament. She'd kicked out with her foot, forcing her opponent to backwing toward her. Serena won that game, but I wasn't going for prizes. I swung a leg toward Boran's face. When he yanked his head back, I whacked him square in the chest with my other heel.

Thrown off balance, Boran floundered, his wings flapping uselessly as he tumbled into the Toos' rainwater pool. When he hit, a huge splash went up. He shrieked and went under.

The Toos' gate guards came running around the back of the villa. Ilyssa shouted, "Hold the guy in the pool. He's a thief." Boran surfaced to find two spears aimed at his head.

Ilyssa touched my face. "Are you all right?" she asked with worry in her eyes.

"Fine," I lied. It took all my willpower to keep from rubbing my sore jaw.

She yelled at Boran, "You're a miserable, mite-bitten excuse for a Mountaineer!" and she snatched up Mellora's bag. Checking inside, she said, "There's my pearl ring, and Sorlyn's—"

Calling Ilyssa's name, Lady Too ran from the villa. She folded Ilyssa in her arms, crying, laughing and scolding at the same time. Honorable Too was right behind her. He took Ilyssa's face in his hands and kissed her forehead. "You were reckless, daughter, to go on such a journey," he said sternly.

"But I'm a champion," Ilyssa replied, as though that explained everything.

Maybe it did. Her parents released her, looked at each other, and sighed. They eyed Boran, now slogging out of the pool. With his feathers drenched and dripping, he looked a lot smaller.

Ilyssa said, "Kor just stopped Boran from stealing from us. Look!" She held up Mellora's bag.

"The aquilan's a looter?" Lady Too glared at Boran. "He said he was checking for unsafe roofs and walls. With so many people around," she gestured to a group of bedraggled-looking Tropicals still in their party clothes who were watching us from the villa's porch, "I forgot he was here."

The guards hadn't. One poked Boran with his spear to keep him from moving closer to us. "Sir, what should we do with this one?" the guard asked.

"Take out the trash," Hon. Too instructed. "Escort him to the gate. Make sure the sentries remember his face. We don't want him coming back to Sea Grove."

I turned to go, but Ilyssa said, "Wait. Mother, Father, this is Kor—"

"Tiercel. Yes, we know," said Hon. Too. "We've heard all about 'Kor, Monster Slayer' from his brother. And that," he pointed to Boran, "was nice work." Ilyssa's father smiled and raised his fist in greeting. "Aurelius Too. We owe you a great debt for saving our daughter."

Other than the Grays, I'd never had a grown-up Tropical talk to me before, let alone know my name. We touched fists. Ilyssa started describing other things I'd done. Lady Too cut in to ask if Mellora was safe, and then Ilyssa wanted to know about her sister, who was helping out in the grove somewhere. "With her fiancé and no chaperone," Ilyssa's mother moaned. "What are things coming to?"

Then Lady Too said to me, "I'm sorry we're not prepared to entertain you properly at the moment. Our guests stayed here during the entire siege." She confided in a whisper, "Coming from the empire's capital, they're used to servants doing *everything*. The villa's a mess. We're sending them to lodge with friends while we neaten things up." In a louder voice, she said, "We'd be so pleased if you could visit us tomorrow."

I opened my mouth, but nothing came out.

Ilyssa laughed. "He certainly will, Mother. If he's going escort me to Sorlyn's wedding feast, I'll have to teach him to dance."

"*Dance?*" I croaked. I imagined dancing as the Tropicals did, touching hands, bodies close. I thought about me, a Woodlander, with Ilyssa Too as my partner. I stared down at my big feet.

Hon. Too cleared his throat. "Dancing lessons can wait. You've earned some time off. You should relax, enjoy the last of the warm weather. I've saved a jug of mango juice, and we'll get the pool cleaned even if we have to do it ourselves."

Lady Too cried, "Aurelius!"

Ilyssa's father chuckled. He clapped me on the shoulder. I noticed he had to reach up to do that. "Go home, lad. Get some rest. Remind Elder Tiercel not to be late for the meeting tomorrow. We have a lot to get through."

Elder Tiercel? When had my father become a council member? What else had changed while we were gone? Remembering that we still had to tell the Council of Elders about Chip and his people, I knew Ilyssa was right: Things would never be the same.

Then I thought about tomorrow, when I'd be sipping mango juice in the rainwater pool with Ilyssa. I was going to like the new Sea Grove. I was going to like it a lot.

ABOUT THE AUTHOR

"Reality can be beaten with enough imagination."—Mark Twain

Sanna Hines loves writing about people whose lives are changing. What better way to discover your true self than to experience a perilous adventure?

Sanna and her family undertook their own adventure when they moved to Maine in 2016. Living in a house more than two centuries old is just the thing to inspire imagination.

Learn more at

Sanna Hines' Worlds http://sannahines.wixsite.com/sanna-hines-worlds

Another World https://sannahines.wordpress.com/

Amazon https://www.amazon.com/Sanna-Hines/e/B011HCBJPE

Facebook https://www.facebook.com/sanna.hines.author

Goodreads https://www.goodreads.com/author/show/14050716.Sanna_Hines

Twitter @sannahines1

All reviews are greatly appreciated.

ALSO BY SANNA HINES

STEALTH MOVES
Young Adult Thriller

When Beacon Hill preppie Liv Smallwood sees her classmate kidnapped, she launches a campaign to draw all of Boston into the search. Holly Glasscock, bodyguard, must keep Liv from the man who calls himself "Stealth," a man tormented by the death of his twin brother, Brandon. Stealth will do anything to appease Brandon, even risk a final, desperate capture.

https://www.amazon.com/Stealth-Moves-Sanna-Hines
ebook/dp/B00ZXYFEZY

Shining Ones: Legacy of the Sidhe
Irish Fantasy Adventure

Born a descendant of Ireland's magical *Tuatha dé Danann*, police officer Tessa Holly will never grow sick or old. When her brother and a human girl are seized by enemies, Tessa must rely on a man no one trusts as her guide through Ireland and Britain in search of her people's greatest treasures.

https://www.amazon.com/Shining-Ones-Legacy-Sanna-Hines-
ebook/dp/B018EJ8EJ2

Elvira Wonders
Paranormal Mystery

Elvira is home to creatures the world doesn't want—or wants too much, like the fairies. Now tourists are coming to see the wonders. Before they arrive, someone starts stalking the town's star attractions. Ghost hunter Josh Seldom and his (mostly human) friends must stop the mayhem. But in a town full of monsters, how do you find a killer?

https://www.amazon.com/Elvira-Wonders-Sanna-Hines-
ebook/dp/B07693L4NS

www.ingramcontent.com/pod-product-compliance
Lightning Source LLC
Chambersburg PA
CBHW030615130626
46552CB00002B/582